Journey Through a Labyrinth

The Memoirs of Emma Fiedler

A Novel by Arletta Lowe Case

Journey Through a Labyrinth is a work of fiction and not meant as a source to document research. Some characters and incidents are based on historical records, but much of the content is the creation of the author's imagination.

What is this mighty labyrinth—the earth,
But a wild maze the moment of our birth?
— *British Magazine* for 1747

⌲ A NOTE TO READERS ⌲

For our mother, this book was a work of love. Upon a trip to New Harmony, Indiana, she became intrigued with what life would have been like in the 1800s for a young girl growing up there. She kept returning with family and friends and began to do research in earnest to begin writing this book. *A Journey Through the Labyrinth* became her passion, and it was finished just prior to her death.

Seeing this book put into print is a labor of love by us, her children, to honor our mother and make her wish come true. We hope you enjoy reading it as much as she enjoyed writing it.

The Case Family

⚒ ACKNOWLEDGMENTS ☞

I will always remember Dawn Priest, a volunteer tourist guide at New Harmony, Indiana. When this book was just an idea, she showed interest, sent me information and offered encouragement. Because my professional expertise was nonfiction, I enrolled in The Institute of Children's Literature, a correspondence school, and was lucky enough to be assigned to Patricia Viglucci with her unending patience. I also took a helpful online fiction writing class sponsored by Indiana State University. Their archives department was helpful in clarifying facts as was the special collections section at the Vigo County Library. At the beginning of this endeavor, my book was to be about a little girl, and Stan Evans, who taught a class in children's literature at Indiana State University, was kind enough to allow me to audit his class. Stan read the bare bones beginning of my book and offered a critique. My book, however, evolved from children's literature to adult. A good friend, Joan Overpeck, provided invaluable help with her line by line analysis and detailed, written comments as this work progressed.

Members of my writers' club offered insight and editing, especially Judy Francis, who stayed in touch even after the club disbanded. Kay Harper, a former colleague, who used to take students on field trips to New Harmony, was kind enough to accompany me to New Harmony on one of my visits. She came along at a time when I needed my memory refreshed with the history of the area. Heartfelt thanks goes to Jennifer Minigh, family friend and owner of Shade Tree Publishing in West Virginia. Although she deals exclusively with nonfiction, she took her time to read the manuscript and offer her insights. Thanks to Sandy Ferguson Fuller and Lynn Volkens. They found empty spots that needed to be filled. Ken Couch, the computer specialist at Sackrider and Company, kept my computer healthy and saved my day more than once. My son was my adviser when my memory could not come up with specifics regarding farming, farm animals, and hunting. My daughter Brenda, an avid reader, was one of my advisers and sometimes a typist. My Texas relatives lent encouragement beyond measure. And for any other friends and acquaintances that helped in any way during this undertaking, please know that you are appreciated.

Arletta L. Case

❧ INTRODUCTION ☞

The Harmonist Society that established towns in Pennsylvania and Indiana was founded by George Rapp, who had belonged to a church in Württemberg, a province in southwest Germany. He began to question some of the doctrines of that church and discussed it with other parishioners. They agreed with him. Eventually they left the church and began to assemble in their respective homes. They were ordered to disband their private meetings and when they did not, Rapp and some of the others were imprisoned for a brief time. After their release, dissension mounted, and they began making plans to go to America where they would have freedom to worship without the shackles of religious and governmental control.

⚞ The Journal of Emma Fiedler ⚟

I called him the Memory-keeper. He came uninvited and infringed upon my thoughts during occasional sleepless nights and sometimes during my leisure moments of the day.

Sometimes he came cloaked in dark obscurity, hinting at things best left alone, but other times he gave me the gift of a smile. Revelations from the Memory-keeper came at his will and only in bits and pieces. He never revealed a complete story. I wanted to know the complete story, so I began to ask questions of everyone I knew and wrote what they told me along with what I remembered myself.

My name is Emma Fiedler, and the following is the story of my life as true as it can ever be known.

PART I

❧ Summer 1804 ❧

On Board the Aurora

The man with the deep raspy voice had told me to stay put. I think that was what he told me. He was waving his arms and shouting at everyone scrunched together in the filth and darkness of the hold. But during the mayhem and weeping, I crept up the ladder and crouched behind a stack of crates as I had done the day before.

Papa said German people love flowers and music so much because they both lift the spirits. So I tried to remember what the flowers in Wurttemberg smelled like, what they looked like, but I couldn't. I tried to remember the tune to *Es Bluht ein Blumlein*. The song is about flowers, and I wanted to sing it, right then, for Papa. But the cold gray dampness of the sea air closed in on me and swallowed my soul.

Papa always said that death was only the beginning of a new life. That did not comfort me as I saw one body after another slip over the rail and enter the dark water with a dreadful splash. I didn't even know which body was Papa's. At least yesterday Mama was the only one. "Mama, this is Emma," I had whispered as she disappeared. "Enjoy your new life."

Our ship, the *Aurora*, docked in Baltimore in the late summer of 1804. As the passengers disembarked, a woman I didn't know saw my wide-eyed fear and the trails my tears had made when they trickled down my face through the dirt. She grabbed my hand as we were pushed along with the crowd.

When there was space to breathe, she asked, "Where are your parents, little one?"

I pointed to the ocean.

"You stay close to us," the woman said. Then she whispered, "What is your name?"

"Emma," I whispered back.

When it was our turn to answer the questions of the port authorities, the man with her answered, "I'm Yurgen Fiedler and this is my wife, Gerta."

"And the little girl?"

The man wore a puzzled expression on his face.

Gerta quickly stepped forward. "Emma. Emma Fiedler," she answered.

I was not quite five years old, and that was my first step in becoming the Fiedler's adopted child.

❧ Winter 1804 ❧

Baltimore

Most of our people stayed in the East working on farms throughout Maryland while George Rapp, our leader, and a small group of men left to search for land on which we could permanently settle and build a new life. They purchased a tract they liked in Butler County, Pennsylvania, and began to clear the land and build shelters. Those of us who had stayed behind were soon called together and instructed to begin the journey to our new location. Some, however, had already put down roots and stayed where they were, but the rest of us left in the middle of winter so we could reach Butler County in time for spring planting. The winter was harsh during the three hundred mile trip by horses and Conestoga-type wagons. Eventually supplies ran low and the people were hungry and cold. Some died.

Against all odds, Gerta had given birth to Gustav, a healthy baby boy, shortly after we arrived in Baltimore. Although Gus, as they called him, was robust, Gerta's strength had been depleted. Everybody helped. They carried the baby and sometimes they almost carried Gerta, who stumbled and fell frequently. At first she tried to refuse the help, but as the journey continued, she didn't even have the strength to do that. Finally, because of the dwindling supplies, there was room for her in one of the wagons.

As soon as we were close enough to our destination, one of the men rode ahead to fetch Dr. Christoph Mueller from the new settlement site. He and some of the others came back with food and blankets for everyone and healing herbs for Gerta.

"Thank you, Christoph. God bless you." Yurgen couldn't utter another word. As I saw him brush the tears from his eyes, I began to cry too.

"Come here, little one," Yurgen told me. "Don't be afraid. We'll be all right now."

❧ Spring 1814 ❧

Pennsylvania

Our settlement in Butler County was named Harmonie and given the German spelling. I think this was to help us remember our German heritage. Father Rapp believed if they had harmony in their new location, the settlement would definitely be successful. It was organized according to teachings in the Bible. One verse they relied on was in Acts 4:32.

All the believers were one in heart and mind.

No one claimed that any of his possessions was his own,

but they shared everything they had.

The community prospered. In only ten years it grew from nothing into a town that had streets, brick houses, community stores, and everything else one would expect. In fact it soon outgrew its location, and our leaders sold that tract of land and the buildings and made plans to move.

Father Rapp thought we needed room for expansion, a better climate in which to grow grapes and citrus, and a waterway for easier shipping. He found a place in the triangle of the Ohio and Wabash Rivers in southwest Indiana. He told them he knew the land would be good because there were black locust trees along the streams. He announced that his people were being called to move again. As before, a small group went ahead to start clearing the land and building shelters for the others who would follow later.

My best friend, Katerina, was the only one to hear my complaints. "Although I was quite young," I reminded her, "I remember that frightening trip with the snow and icy wind pelting us in the face. And of course I remember the ten long years of hard work building our town. You remember, Kat. And now we're going to do the whole thing over again? I'm happy here. I don't want to go. Do you?"

Kat said nothing but when I turned to look at her, I knew the answer. She didn't want to go either. I wondered how many others felt the same. But we did go. We had no choice.

PART II

❧ Spring 1814 ❧

Indiana

As if rafting down the swift-flowing Ohio River then poling up the muddy Wabash weren't bad enough, fighting my way through the weeds, brush, and briars of the Indiana wilderness was even worse. Having the first view of my new home was the final insult. I knew the dwelling was to be temporary, but unless temporary meant only one day from sunup to sundown, it was too long. There before me was a tiny, ugly one-room shelter with dirt for a floor. Visions of the beautiful house I had left behind in Pennsylvania flashed before my eyes. I remembered its beautiful yard with flowers and herbs, its basement with wonderful foods stored there, and its upstairs with two bedrooms. I also remembered the town, clean and organized. As an act of frustration, I reached for the hunting knife Papa had left on the rough hewn table and sliced off my long blond braids, the long hair that is the crowning glory of any devout Harmonist woman.

"Oh, Emma! What happened?" Gus asked as he suddenly appeared in the doorway and saw me holding one of the braids I had just detached from my head. "Did you do that?"

I nodded.

"You mustn't let Mama and Papa see you like this. Why did you do it?" Then without waiting for an answer, although he was only ten, my younger brother took charge. "Crates are still stacked in that clearing where they were unloaded. I'll sneak down there and see if I can find a sewing basket. Maybe we can sew your braids back on."

"We can't sew hair back on. It has to grow back."

"Oh, yes. I do know that, Emma. But doesn't it take a long time?" asked Gus.

"Yes, I'm afraid it does," I told him. I pressed my hands to my throat when I realized what I had done. I knew Mama and Papa would both be very disappointed in me. "We can't sew hair back on, but maybe we can sew the braids to my skull cap. We can tuck the cut ends under the cap and sew them in place. Maybe it won't be noticed. Yes, please try to find a sewing basket."

When Mama and Papa came, they were loaded down with stacks of blankets and baskets full of utensils and other necessities. They sent Gus and me back down by the river to get another load.

"They didn't notice," Gus said. "We did a good job."

"They weren't looking. They were too busy," I replied.

I was almost running. Although a briar caught my skull cap, yanked it sideways, and scratched my face, I didn't stop. "Hurry Gus. Get as much as you possibly can carry and hurry."

Mama looked up as we came in. "Emma, put those..." Her voice trailed off. For a moment she stood in stunned silence. Then, holding to the table, she lowered herself onto a chair. Papa turned to see why the activity had stopped abruptly.

"Gerta, do you need to rest a spell?" he asked as he straightened up from shoving crates over to the wall. His eyes followed Mama's gaze. Then sounds such as I had never heard from him filled the little room. Indiscernible sounds. Something from the Old Country perhaps. Maybe a desperate prayer. Finally he tried to speak. "What hap...?" He stopped and looked again at Mama for some kind of a clue.

I have never again experienced a silence as deep or long as in that little room. An eternity it seemed. And as I remember it, no one was breathing.

Mama was first to break the horrible silence. "Emma, you have a braid that seems to be growing out of your ear," she stammered.

I reached up and felt for my cap. The bramble that had caught my skull cap had pulled it to the side putting the attached braid right over my ear.

"Come here," Mama whispered.

She carefully removed my cap which included the braids sewn to the underside. My chopped hair was revealed in all its ugliness. I think Mama was in too much pain to comment. When I turned to look at Papa, his drawn white face revealed his distress.

"Why Emma? Why did you do such a thing?" Mama asked.

"I don't know," I answered. And that was the truth. I didn't know. To this day I don't really know. But I do remember that when I faced both Mama and Papa, I might have been happy to die just to escape. I wondered, however, if maybe this was so horrible that I would remember it even after death. It wasn't the loss of my hair that was the true issue. It was what my hair stood for, obedience to God. My spiritual obedience to God and my parents.

Papa, his head still lowered, quietly left the little room and walked back toward the river. Mama called to him, but he didn't answer. She hesitated then hurried after him.

That night I tossed and turned in a fitful sleep. My first thought upon waking was the loss of my hair. My second thought was facing Mama and Papa again. I wondered whether things would ever be normal again. I wondered if Mama and Papa would be sorry they had kept me.

✦ Spring 1815 ✦

My hair grew out in the year since I impulsively whacked it off. My braids had grown out, and I had grown up, at least a little. Neither Mama nor Papa had mentioned my barbering experiment since the day it happened. Surprisingly, neither had Gus. Forgiveness is an important Harmonist belief, and it had been given to me freely.

I picked up my journal that had slipped to the floor when I fell asleep the previous night. I started to return it to its hiding place but noticed a poem I scarcely remembered writing. I had been thinking about the labyrinth at the edge of our Pennsylvania village. Father Rapp had often told us that life is just like searching for a path through a labyrinth. He said that we take many wrong turns when trying to find the temple in the center. So we have to go back and try again and again and again. I had written:

The Labyrinth

A child in Time and Spirit

I wandered among deceiving pathways

wounded by thorns

frightened by night sounds

confused by a hedge-row maze

Always searching for the temple

of harmony in the center.

There was no time for frittering. I could hear Mama working in the kitchen, and my day begins helping her. I knew that if I were late to help, Papa would say, "Emma, it's hard to stir porridge from upstairs."

I quickly secured my journal, splashed cold water on my face from the basin by my bed, washed my hands with the bit of lye soap in the little dish, grabbed my clothes from the pegs on the wall, and dressed hurriedly.

I loved our new house. It was exactly like the one we had left behind. Building it was a relatively easy task since all the boards were precut from a previous design and labeled with Roman numerals so they could quickly be put into their proper places. It had a wide entry hall, a common room, and a kitchen downstairs. Another wide hall separated two bedrooms upstairs. We still had much to do, however, before we could call this new place a town. At least it had a name, it was Harmonie with the German spelling, just like the town we left behind. We looked forward to the arrival of another boatload of immigrants to provide more help.

I climbed up on the wooden bench in front of the window at the end of the hall to look out at the awakening spring. There is nothing like nature in the spring. The birds were chirping, the grass was greening, the naked branches of the redbuds and dogwoods were blossoming. The cycle of seasons. Always in harmony.

I bounded down the stairs, tying my skull cap under my chin as I went, and hurried into the common room where the rest of the family was seated for breakfast. My mama's spicy boiled sausage smelled wonderful. She said nothing about my tardiness, but Papa said, "You need to move with more quietness, Emma."

"Yes, Papa," I answered and slid into my place and bowed my head for the blessing. I knew it would be short and to the point. Papa never wasted anything, not even words.

"Vater Gott," he said, "see us through this day according to Thy will. Amen."

After breakfast Papa sat down in the common room and removed a shoe. "My big toe just came out for air, Gerta," he said.

"Get one of your other socks, and I'll get that one darned today," Mama answered.

There were always enough socks since one of our factories made them. Some were made of wool from our own sheep, but for warmer weather, they were made of cotton which was grown on our own land. I remember a story I heard about a visitor who came to see how our Society was organized and during part of his tour he was taken to see the factories. Frederick was the escort, and at one stop the women workers asked him if they could sing for the visitor. He agreed so work was briefly stopped. The visitor was quite impressed with the work, the singing, and the flowers that were at every station.

"Things are going well. The Society has nine thousand pounds of pork in the smokehouse," Papa said. "It will sell for three or three and a half cents a pound. We only lost a few lambs; we have over two hundred alive and well."

"I heard Frederick say that a place in Kentucky ordered one hundred cows," Gus added.

"Yes. And all skins are plentiful; a raccoon skin is now twenty-five cents," Papa said.

"We are truly blessed," Mama answered.

Papa headed toward the barn, and Gus got ready for school. "When Frederick came back from Vincennes, he brought a new boy with him," Gus told us.

Hopefully, the boy would be of some help with construction even if he had never seen a nail or a board. We needed those two boatloads of immigrants to arrive soon.

I cornered Gus as soon as I could. "What does that new boy look like, Gus?"

"As it happens, he's not a boy, Em. He's a grown man."

"Well, whatever he is, what does he look like?"

"I didn't look at him close, but I could tell that he had two arms, two legs, one nose..."

Suddenly Gus dodged a basin of dirty dish water as he went down the steps and into the yard, and I was determined to learn to throw straighter.

He was laughing. "Is that any way for you to behave?" he called back.

"When I have a brother like you, any behavior is acceptable."

"Emma, are you talking to someone?" Mama called from upstairs.

"No. Only Gus and he's leaving."

"Well, call to him," Mama said. "Finish cleaning the dishes, then you can walk with him as far as the Schaefer's house and fetch the child back here. Except for him, the entire family is sick."

"What's wrong?"

"Malaria maybe."

"Malaria! Are they sure?"

"No, dear girl, I said maybe. We will think good thoughts not bad ones. Besides I really think it's too early in the season for malaria."

My mind wasn't on cleaning the dishes. I was remembering our arrival at the new settlement last year. We had such poor accommodations. The brothers had broken up the flat boats they arrived on and used the lumber to construct temporary dwellings for those who would come later. We were lucky to get one of those. There wasn't enough lumber, so some folks lived in sod houses and during the rainy season, the sod got damp as did the dirt floors. The standing water throughout the area bred swarms of mosquitoes that spread beyond control. The Peruvian bark that Christoph used to treat the sick seemed to help some, but even with that, many of our people died of malaria.

"Finally ready I see," Gus said as he stood up from where he sat on the bottom step waiting for me.

"I wish I were going to school. I really miss it," I responded.

"I know you do. It's not fair to have to quit school just because you turned fourteen. Especially when you really like to go. As for me, I could care less. There's Will," he said as he pointed toward the garden. With a quick wave to the little boy, he continued on his way.

I turned toward the Schaefer house. The morning sun filtered through the leaves and wrapped Will in its light as he sat alone on a bench swinging his legs. He looked like a little angel.

Willem was Kat's little brother. Kat was my age, fifteen, and Will was much younger. He was two. In the Society, celibacy was encouraged but not demanded. The encouragement did not work for everyone, Kat's parents among them.

While we were still in Pennsylvania, some of the people brought up the subject of celibacy, and thought it would bring them closer to God as the Bible said. They wanted to observe that rule. That meant couples who were already married would now live as brothers and sisters. They could then have their mind on spiritual things instead of physical things.

Another argument for celibacy was entirely practical. If a woman had a child, her time would be taken up with domestic things for the family. She could not go to the fields or the factories to work and help build the community. As for me, I'm glad celibacy is optional. Otherwise, we would not have Will.

Kat called from the open window upstairs where she had been trying to keep an eye on her active brother. "Hello, Em. Thanks for taking Will. Be good, Will."

Will gave a quick glance toward Kat and waved goodbye. "I caught a widdle fwog, Em," he announced with great pride.

"Umm," I responded. I had sensed a forced lightheartedness in Kat's voice and tried to match the tone when I called back. "You'll get well quick, Kat. I know it."

Will was tugging at my arm. "The fwog wants to skip, Em," he said.

I took Will's hand and skipped with him down the street.

"Mama!" I called as we entered the house. "Will's here."

Mama appeared just as Will extracted the frog from his pocket and held it facing him. Both of his little hands encircled the frog just under its front legs. Those two legs stuck straight out and left the two hind legs dangling. Will put his nose against the frog's nose and said affectionately, "Hehwo, my widdle man."

I burst out laughing. "He does look somewhat like a little man," I said. "The frog, I mean."

"Ach da! Oh, my!" Mama exclaimed, her eyes never leaving the creature suspended in midair. She tried not to smile.

"Don't let him kiss that frog anymore, Emma," she said. "Will, don't kiss the frog any more."

"Why not, Gerta?"

"It makes them angry and sad; anyway, it causes some kind of a problem. Do you want to take the child for a walk down to the pond?" Mama asked me. "That will occupy him for a spell and give me a chance to catch up on my work."

"Come on, Will. Let's take Frog for a walk. We'll put him in this little basket. It can be his house. You might find some pretty rocks down at the branch."

I liked the branch, a little tributary that angled off from the river, made an S-curve, then rejoined the river farther downstream. Because one of the S-curves was blocked by fallen trees and branches, it flowed slowly and formed a pond. Fishing was good here, and somewhere close to this location, the bank had washed away from the roots of a large tree which then had fallen into the water. It supposedly made such a big splash that it washed a large fish weighing several pounds up onto the bank. Whoever was present had a lot of fish for supper. If I think about it, I must ask Gus who that was.

I sat down on a log that had a limb attached at an angle, which made a perfect backrest. It was a wonderful spot: in the shade, off the ground, and in sight of Will. Every time Will found a rock, he brought it to show me. "Look, Emma, look. Here's another pwetty one. Is this pink?" he asked, pointing to a little streak on the side.

"No, that's blue. See, this is pink," I said, picking up one of the other rocks and showing him its pink speckles.

"Oh, my! There goes Frog. He's headed for the pond! Stay here, Will. I'll get him!" The leaves, sheltered from the sun and still wet from the morning dew, seemed as slick as winter ice. As I tried to run I slid, fell, righted myself, and plunged ahead. I tried as hard as I could, but I was too late. The frog reached the bank, gathered his hind legs under him, then stretched himself out to his full length in a jump for his freedom. As he was about to kersplash into the pond, a bass jumped and with wide open mouth made the frog his dinner.

I turned to look at Will. His eyes were wide and puzzled. "Whez Fwog?" he asked.

"He had an accident," I told him. "The fish swallowed him."

"Is he dead?"

"Yes, Will, he is."

"Is he in heaven?"

I had no idea how to answer his question. I did not believe that frogs went to heaven, but how would I explain that to a little boy who thought the frog was a person? I paused, then said, "Yes, Will, he's in heaven." Will nodded. I was relieved that he seemed satisfied with the explanation.

Will was pleasant and fun on the way home. Mama and Papa were almost ready for supper when we came in. I helped Will wash up at the wash basin and found him a place at the table. He ate heartily. As we were leaving the table, he turned and announced in a jovial manner, "Fwog had an accident and died. He went up to heaven." Startled, everyone looked up, but before anyone could comment, Will turned to me and said, "I don't want him to be up there any longer, Em. I'm ready for him to come back now."

———•+•———

We were all anxious for news about Kat and her family. Mama was busy and Papa was gone, so I volunteered to take Will with me to Christoph's office to find out. I rejoiced when I found out that they did not have malaria. Their illness was an ailment in their chests that could be treated with Christoph's herbal medicines.

"You can take Will home this evening or tomorrow or whenever you're ready," Christoph told me. "I was going to send John with a message," he added.

"John?" I asked.

"He came back from Vincennes with Frederick," he said.

"Gus mentioned something about that," I replied. "I think while Will and I are out, I will take him for a short walk. Mama says being outside helps get rid of some of his energy."

I loved to be outside every chance I could manage. Down toward the river it began to get muddy, and we turned to go back but not before I noticed an assortment of wild flowers that sculpted a rainbow of colors at the edge of the tree line.

"Look at those pretty flowers, Will. Wouldn't a bouquet of those look pretty on the tables in the orchard?"

"Let's get some," he squealed and made a dive toward the tree line. He only got one foot in the mud before I scooped him up and put him back on dry land.

When we got home, our family was glad to hear the good news about the Schaefers. I told them about the flooded lowlands and muddy creek bottoms. "Our town is on higher ground. We'll be all right," Mama replied.

"There certainly is a great deal of standing water. Lots of puddles. Everything seems to be wet."

"Including Will," Mama observed. "Not only wet but muddy. Come with me into the kitchen Will, and I'll put you into the tub. You look as if you've been helping the men dig the drainage ditch. Have you?"

"No, Gerta," he answered, shaking his head vigorously. "I've been with Em. Haven't I, Em? Haven't I been with you?"

"Oh, yes. I must have forgotten," Mama told him.

Mama almost always had hot water in the stove's reservoir, and today was no different. She took the oak tub down from a peg on the wall, put in the water and then Will. She soaped up a cloth and began the task of making Will clean again before we took him home.

"Oh! You're hahting my young skin," he complained. Mama flashed me a smile over Will's head.

"Your young skin? I guess we do often tell you that you are too young, too young to go with Gus, too young to go to the river by yourself."

"Too young to climb that big oak," I interrupted.

"Yes, that's right, but your skin is not too young to get washed," Mama smiled.

"Ouch!" Will answered. Then he added, "Mama and Papa and Kat are all well. I'm going home soon, aren't I, Em? Aren't I going home soon?"

"Yes, and I'm going to miss you. I think I will cry and cry."

"No, Em. Don't do that. You will make more muddy puddles, and Gerta will have to scrub you, too."

———·•·———

I waited a few days and then I walked down to check on the Schaefer family. Kat was following Christoph's orders to sit out in the sun as much as possible. She had spread a cover on the ground and Will was sitting with her. Will suddenly jumped up.

"A bunny babbit. Look, Kat!" Will squealed.

I saw the rabbit run through the yard and go under the large mound of limbs that had been deposited by the wind and stacked by children after school.

Will had a language all his own, and I loved it. "I saw it," I told him. "I love bunnies. I think they're sweet. Just like you."

"I'm not a bunny, Em. I'm a widdle boy."

"You hop around like a bunny sometimes."

"Like this?" Will asked. He dropped to all fours and gave an awkward imitation of a rabbit. Mostly his front stayed in one place, and his legs kicked up and down which caused him to fall over from time to time.

Kat and I were laughing when a male voice behind us asked, "What have we here?"

"We have a hopping bunny babbit," Kat answered.

I turned to see who belonged to the deep voice. He was tall and muscular with dark wavy hair, dark deep set eyes, and a smile that lit up all of Harmonie. His clothes marked him as someone outside the Society. Suddenly, it struck me. The new man. The one who came from Vincennes with Frederick.

"Isn't your name John?" Kat asked.

"Yes, and your name is?"

"I'm Katerina Schaefer. My friends call me Kat. The performing bunny is my brother, Will, and this is Emma Fiedler."

I still had not said a word. I could hardly breathe.

"Are you Gus's sister?" he asked me.

I think I answered. Maybe I just nodded. My head was spinning. I wondered what was wrong with me. If this feeling didn't go away, I would have to consult Christoph tomorrow. Maybe he could give me a tonic to take away this strange feeling.

"Where's Gus?" John asked.

I finally found my voice. "He's in school," I answered.

"Why aren't you in school, Emma?"

"We don't go to school after we turn fourteen," I replied.

"And are you saying that you are past fourteen?"

"I'm past fifteen," I said, trying not to sound indignant. I wanted to ask him why he wasn't in school, although he was obviously beyond school age.

"My, fifteen and no bigger than a cricket," he said with a quirky twinkle in his eyes. Then he suddenly changed the subject. "I need to go. I'm glad to meet all of you. Especially the bunny." He smiled and leaned down to acknowledge Will, who developed a sudden case of shyness and tried to wrap himself up in Kat's skirt. We silently watched John until he was out of sight.

Finally Kat said, "He seems nice enough. Even if he isn't one of us. Don't you think so?"

"He's as much one of us as anyone," I answered. "Why does everyone have to fit a pattern? Maybe we should just stuff people into a mold like we do when we pour wax to make candles."

"Oh, Em. You know what I mean."

"I'm sorry, Kat. I don't know what's wrong with me. I need to go home. I must be tired. I'll probably see you tomorrow. I think our mothers have been assigned the same time at the community ovens, so I'll see you then."

When I got home, Mama was cleaning the top of our kitchen stove while it was cool. It was an iron stove that was heated with wood or coal, and it sat on four legs which rested in a tray of sand for protection in case hot coals popped out. The stove had an oven, but when baking several pies or several loaves of bread, we used the large stone ovens spaced throughout the town. I knew that tomorrow we would be baking at the community oven on our street.

Eventually I would do the baking by myself. I knew how to mix and knead the dough and cover it to let it rise, but testing the oven was a dreaded chore. Mama started a new fire with small limbs. When the fire burned down, she scraped out the ashes and used a pole to push a wet rag back and forth to clean the oven's floor. Then she tested the heat by holding her hand inside to the count of twenty to see if the heat was right to bake loaves with a nice brown crust. Next she put each puffy loaf onto a paddle that had a long handle, eased the paddle into the oven, then carefully slid the loaf off onto the brick floor.

Because of my rambling thoughts, it wasn't until I got home did I realize that I hadn't even said goodbye to Will who was still wrapped up in Kat's frock.

❧ Spring 1816 ❧

This morning Mama had been working in the herbs that were always planted behind the flower garden. She was now close to the doorsteps planting tansy to keep the flies away as she always had done. She wore her usual white skullcap fitted across the crown of her head and a long, dull grey dress covered by a bib apron as she always had done. All the women and girls wore the same kind of frock every day. Everything was being done as it always had been done. Everything was so predictable.

As far as the men were concerned, if you saw them from the back you could scarcely tell one from another. They all wore loose plain trousers with grey muslin shirts and long coats called surtouts. Sometimes they wore the famous Harmonist jeans. The outfit was completed by small crowned hats with large brims. I was thinking about all this sameness when Mama's voice startled me.

"Are you finished with all your chores yet, Emma?" she asked.

"Yes, Mama," I said, "I'm finished. I'll stop for Kat as I go by, and we'll go to the field together."

"I'll see all of you at *vesper brodt*," Mama answered.

I was always grateful for *vesper brodt*, our mid-morning and mid-afternoon snacks. We worked hard and the cider and homemade bread with butter gave us a restful break, especially needed by Papa and Gus. They had been up since five o'clock getting seed ready for planting.

Kat was leaving her house when I got there. I waved at Will who was standing in the doorway watching us leave. "Don't be too friendly," she said. "He's already asked a hundred times if he can go with us."

"That will never change. I think he will always want to go with us. Kat, have you noticed that nothing changes around here?"

"Nothing changes? I don't know what you mean. Of course things change around here. Lots of things have changed, Em. This was once a wilderness. Look at it now. We have fields and fields of grain, rows of fruit trees, lovely family houses, dormitories for single people and those couples who wish to live as single people. We will soon have a self-sufficient town. I can think of another change, John came here to live. I think you're quite fond of him."

"He's a friend, I guess. I'm fond of all my friends. So yes, I guess that means I'm fond of him."

I was glad we were interrupted by the sound of the band. It seemed to me that there was music everywhere in our Harmonist Society. Now the band was leading the workers to the field. The men went first, then the women, and then the young people and children. They were on South Street heading toward Main. Some of the women were hurrying to catch up to the others and talking among themselves.

"It vunders me how the fields all planted vill get," said Gretchen Dittmar.

"Yah, the rain in floods is comes often much," answered Elsa Eckert.

"Hello, Gretchen. Hello, Elsa. You're doing well with your English," I told them.

Relatively new to the Society, these women were trying hard to learn English. English, German and French were taught in the school, and extra English classes were held in the evenings. That encouraged the adults to learn along with their children.

When we arrived at the field, each worker was filling a cloth seed bag with seeds and positioning it on the left hip. The bag was secured by a cloth strap that went up over the right shoulder and down diagonally across their back to fasten to the bag on its reverse side.

"Soon is coming more rain, yah," said Gretchen glancing skyward.

Elsa voiced her agreement.

Kat and I picked up our bags, filled them, and joined the group. We formed a straight line and walked across the field holding the bags open with our left hand so we could scatter the seeds with our right.

Because so many in the Society took part in the planting, it was finished by noon in time for us to return home for lunch. This was not the only field; there would be other fields on other days. As we headed home, John came up beside us.

"Hello, John," said Kat. "I'll see you later, Em. I have to run an errand before I go home."

"What do you have to do?" I asked. Ignoring or not hearing me, Kat turned down a side street.

I glanced at John as I quickly tried to stuff stray strands of hair up under my cap. "I look like a wreck," I announced.

"You could never look like a wreck, Cricket."

"I've gotten used to that nickname, but I can't imagine why. Do you remember when I was fifteen and you told me I was no bigger than a cricket. I thought you meant I looked like a scrawny bug and it hurt my feelings. I thought you didn't like me."

"Now, how could anyone not like you?"

"Don't you think I've grown up in the last two years?"

"You've grown up," John agreed matter-of-factly.

His eyes met mine and lingered for the briefest time before he abruptly lowered his gaze. I heard Gus calling. Maybe if I ignored him, he would go away. But John stopped to wait for Gus, so I did too.

"Hello, John," Gus said. "Are you as tired as I am?"

"Gus wants to hurry me along just so he can eat, don't you Gus?" I asked.

"Yes. I need food. Food!" Gus leaned against me and feigned near loss of consciousness, and I roughly pushed him away. "You see how she cares," Gus moaned.

"See you later." John smiled and shook his head in mock exasperation before he turned toward the Muellers where he spent much of his time helping Christoph. He also helped Frederick and Solomon sometimes, as well as anyone else who needed help.

Frederick Rapp, Father Rapp's adopted son and the Society's business manager, had needed extra help recently. He was elected as a delegate to the Indiana Constitutional Convention and with that came extra duties. John was able to step into some of Frederick's more mundane jobs, which saved some time, and that was helpful. One person, no matter how skilled, can only do so much in a day. My mind seemed to have a habit of dwelling on John and his life. Sometimes I became annoyed with myself.

The first thing I did when I got home was to dash to the little basin on the wash stand inside the kitchen door. We all used the same basin, and the first one there got the clean water.

Gus had stopped at the barn. When he came in, he went to the wash stand. He looked in the basin. He looked at me. I smiled my sweetest smile.

We joined Mama and Papa at the table. A few words were spoken, but when Papa bowed his head, all talking stopped. After the prayer we ate our meal in silence, as always.

The lunch today was spaetzel, dumpling-like noodles, cooked with beef. There were potatoes, boiled and sprinkled with parsley. Our treat of the day was apple pie made from apples sliced then dried in the sun last year.

After the kitchen chores were done, I went outside where I did my best thinking. I let my thoughts replay my encounter with John in hopes I could understand his true feelings. I wanted to analyze his words, his facial expressions, his demeanor. Franz Hugo strolled up and sat down beside me on the grass. I bombarded him with questions.

"Franz Hugo, John said I could never look like a wreck. Does that mean he thinks I look pretty? He said how could anyone not like me. That doesn't mean he likes me in any special way, does it? He said he noticed that I have grown up. Did he mean that he was glad I had grown up? I wish I knew what he meant by all that. What do you think?"

I had asked important questions, and Franz Hugo, our black and white bobbed-tail cat, that lost most of his tail when the barn door closed before all of him got out, didn't even look up. He had stretched out in the sun and was sound asleep.

❧ Spring 1817 ❧

I had looked forward to this worship day because we were going boating afterwards. We filed silently into the church, the men seating themselves on one side and the women on the other. A platform was across the front. Father Rapp, tall and thin with a long silver beard sat there in a chair behind a desk. He wore his usual linsey woolsey garment and a night cap.

As he did from time to time, he preached today about the children in those Lutheran churches in Germany. It still bothered him that almost all the parents tried to make sure their child had the most costly outfit for the communion service. They looked stylish, but they failed to know anything about the meaning of the ritual. Another thing he mentioned was that the church leaders fed their own fat bellies but forgot about the poor.

Apparently those who set the standards in the churches in Germany had let things get out of control, but that should have no bearing on us here in the Society. That was another life, another country. I realized that Father Rapp probably was warning us not to fall prey to the same behavior.

For the prayer at the end, we remained seated and bent forward until our heads almost touched our knees to show reverence and humility. Then we stood and filed silently out of the building.

On this particular day, after worship ended, we began our walk toward the river to go boating. As always, the musicians were bringing their instruments, and soon their music would echo across the water like magic. I climbed into the first boat with some of the others, settled myself and the basket of food I had carried, and watched as everyone else chose a boat.

Along the east shore, the white dogwood blossoms and the yellow-green leaves of the willows made a beautiful contrast as their limbs swayed gently in the breeze. Farther along the bank were river birch, sweet gums, hackberry and persimmon trees and a ground cover of myrtle. The first boat moved out and the rest followed. Beside me sat Kat and Will. The last boat carried the musicians, Mama and Papa were in front of them, and Gus was somewhere with his friends.

"I like being toward the front, don't you, Kat?" I asked. "The music sounds better."

"I like being anywhere, last or first or in the middle. These times on the river are some of my favorite times no matter what boat I'm in." Kat answered. "Look over there," she said and pointed toward the river bank.

I followed her gaze. Unconcerned by our intrusion, a river otter glided along near the shore. Squirrels chased each other across the ground, up the trees and back down again, chattering noisily as they played. Eventually we came to our little island. The splash of the oars dipping in and out of the water slowed. The sound of the musicians stopped and the twittering of the birds hopping about among the trees took its place.

After we had eaten, Kat joined a group waiting for games to begin. I found a sandy place a little apart from the others where a stand of young river willows had stubbornly pushed their roots beyond the sand and into the soil below. They had formed a living fence that separated me from the rest of the group. I had brought my journal and sketch pad, but at the moment I was engrossed in watching the noisy little paroquets building their nests in hollow trees. They often would lay four or five tiny pale green eggs. Such pretty little birds they were with their yellow-green plumage and the orange fluff of tiny feathers at the top of their curved beak, but there was another side to them. They were destructive to our fruit trees. When the fruit appeared they pecked out the seeds which caused the fruit to rot.

The rustle of bushes and the crack of a twig caught my attention. Maybe a puma was wandering about looking for prey. Maybe a gray wolf. Bears had only recently emerged from hibernation. What would I do if one lumbered out into the open where I sat? It would be hungry and irritable. What if it was a sow with cubs? That would be even worse. Someone always brought a gun along, but even if I screamed, they wouldn't hear me. Gertrude, Father Rapp's granddaughter, and her friend Sibilla were singing and the people were clapping. I could scarcely breathe. Another twig snapped, this time louder and closer. I jumped to my feet.

"I didn't mean to startle you, Emma," Aldo Bonn said as he ducked under a low branch on his way over to where I was sitting.

"Well, you did... You frightened me half to death," I told him.

Aldo doesn't fit in with anyone, but it seems that he always shows up when I least expect it. I have little enough time to spend by myself as it is.

"What are you doing? Sketching? May I see?" he asked.

"I never got to it," I answered, trying to put a lilt in my voice. "I've been watching the birds building their nests, but I was about to leave. I need to find Kat."

"I'll walk with you," he offered.

I was walking as fast as I could, still brushing sand from my clothes, when I saw John headed our way. He looked surprised. "I didn't want you to get left behind, but I see you don't need my help. Hello, Aldo," he said as he turned back toward the boats and the festivities that were drawing to a close.

⇝ Summer 1817 ⇜

Spring crept slowly by. Summer finally came. I saw John but only occasionally and at a distance. He always raised his hand in a casual wave but continued on his way. Sometimes I was sure that he altered his path to avoid me.

Summer was more miserable than usual that year partly because there was a serious drought. We prayed for rain at each service and at home but to no avail. Maybe Papa's prayers should have been longer. "Vater Gott, bless us with rain. Amen," he had said.

Kat and I took Will with us to pick blackberries, but from lack of rain, they were not as big and juicy as usual. It took us longer to fill our buckets. Will had only a few in the bottom of his. One look explained why there were not more. His lips were blue, his teeth were blue, his fingers and fingernails were blue. Where he had swiped at his face, probably to get rid of a bug, he had smeared a broad blue streak from the center of his forehead, across his eye brow and onto his ear lobe.

"Kat, do you remember the day in school when Brother Weingartner showed us a picture of *The Blue Boy* painting? We have our own blue boy, but instead of a blue suit he has a blue face too."

"Turn around Will. Let me see."

Will, in an unusually loud and hurried voice, said, "I heard Mama and Papa talking about a panana. They will put it in the church, they said. I think they said Mama might get to play with it. What is a panana?"

I heard a quiver in Will's voice. I suddenly felt ashamed. It was not like me to tease him. I had hurt his feelings. I seemed to be doing many uncharacteristic things recently.

"Will," I said, "put your berries in my bucket." With great pride he poured the berries from his bucket into mine. He poured them slowly a few at a time, investigating to see how much difference it made, and finally pouring in the rest.

"Will, it's called a piano, not a panana. It's a musical instrument like a horn is a musical instrument. Solomon knows how to make music with a horn, and your mama knows how to make music with a piano. One day soon I'll take you over to the church so you can see it. In the meantime, let's go over there to that sandy spot and I will draw you a picture."

He glanced at the sand drawing. "Where do they blow out the music?" he asked. "It doesn't look like a horn".

"No, it doesn't. Let's just wait until we can go to the church, and I will show you the piano."

He paused briefly in deep thought. Then as if there had been no discussion at all, he announced, "We have two big buckets all the way full now." He held onto my apron and skipped along joyfully, ignoring the fact that his bucket was now completely empty.

When we reached the place where two paths converged, Aldo Bonn stepped into view. "Hello," he said, "I didn't know you were picking berries today. We could have picked together." I said nothing but walked on giving Will my undivided attention.

"Christoph, Gus and John are coming," Kat said.

I turned, but John only briefly acknowledged us and continued on his way.

"Did you have good pickings?" Christoph asked.

"The berries aren't as good as usual," I answered watching John's back disappear from view.

"Like everything else, they need rain," Christoph said. "Give greetings to your folks."

I walked the rest of the way from the Schaefer's with Gus. I gave Mama the bucket. "These berries aren't as nice as usual, not as sweet or juicy and not as big," I told her.

"The pies will not know that, and they will taste just as good," she said. "I will bake two at a community oven tomorrow, and we'll eat the rest of the berries with milk. I used the community kitchen to fix food for supper, but we're going to have a cold lunch, and then we will sit under the oak and listen to the band."

The huge old oak was well-known to all of us. When new people arrived, they sometimes camped out under that tree until housing could be found for them. At other times the band gathered there and as soon as they began to play, people came to listen. And sometimes when it was exceedingly hot, Father Rapp delivered his sermons under the tree. That old oak was special to all of us.

Papa carried the *brellsluhlen* outside for Mama. "This chair will be more comfortable for you than the garden bench, Gerta," he said. We had just painted it with egg shell blue paint. Gus and I had watched the paint being made with its buttermilk base.

We had a lunch of cold beef sandwiches, a small sliver of peach pie, and apple cider. Then we walked over to the old oak. The band was getting ready to play, and people were strolling around looking for a comfortable place on the grass to sit. Everyone was ready to enjoy a brief respite of music and friendship. It was a rest from fighting fires for one thing. We had battled a prairie fire which got dangerously close to the fruit trees. In fact, twice we had to grab empty feed sacks and run with everybody to beat the fire out. Usually, we successfully put it out if we saw it right away and got to it fast. Everything was as dry as a crust of year-old bread.

Then, after all that happened, a sister went to sleep in her chair. Her candle burned down to the table scarf and started a fire. The house and everything in it burned. The only blessing was that the three sisters and their elderly mother escaped. I sometimes dwelled on the fact that only a few things my family had really belonged to us. Almost everything belonged instead to the Society. At a time like this, I realized how wonderful it was for that family. The Society would quickly band together, clear the rubble, rebuild the house, and furnish it from top to bottom. Frugally, but adequately.

❧ Autumn 1817 ❧

I swung my legs over the side of the bed. From the basin on the night stand, I splashed cold water on my face, dressed, and hurried downstairs to help with breakfast.

Mama was standing in the doorway looking out toward the garden. "Look at that," she said quietly. "No artist can paint such beauty."

My gaze followed Mama's. When the sun occasionally pushed its way out from between the fast-moving clouds, it cast shadows that constantly changed the autumn leaves from muted earth tones to shades of brilliant orange, deep crimson, and burnished gold, some accented by lingering streaks of green.

"I love autumn, Emma, don't you? Not only is it lovely to look at, but it's the time when we harvest the fruits of our labor."

"Yes, Mama. I love it too," I told her.

Individuals in the Society were consumed with activity. Like busy ants in well-ordered groups, they scurried about preparing for the approaching winter. As for us, after breakfast Mama and Gus dug our potatoes from the ground, and I gathered and stacked them. Later they would be wiped off, laid out to dry, then stored in the cellar beneath our house, carefully spaced so that air could circulate. Onions would be hung up to dry. After the apples were picked, some would be sliced and spread out in the sun to dry and some would be left whole and packed in barrels between layers of sawdust.

"Ah, the end of the row," I heard Gus moan as he raised both arms and stretched toward the sky to relieve his tense aching muscles.

Mama turned over the last shovelful of potatoes, shrugged her shoulders several times to relieve the stiffness, and said, "Let's go in."

I was ready. Since early morning, except for the short break during *vesper brodt*, we had worked non-stop. Each of us snatched up a share of the final uprooted potatoes and spread them on the ground with the others as we went by.

Just as we got inside, the wind seemed to come out of nowhere. My dress billowed around me and wisps of hair that had worked loose from my braids blew across my face. Standing at the open doorway, I raised my voice to be heard above the whistling and howling of the wind sounds. "Look at the sky. It's turning dark. See, there in the distance?"

"Close the door, Emma. Quick!" Mama shouted as her embroidered table scarf was blown from the table. "Gus, run upstairs and close the windows."

As Gus was coming back, the sound of a bugle echoed through the village, and Mama had a new sense of urgency in her voice. "Grain must still be down. It mustn't get wet. Oh, I wish Yurgen was here and not in Terre Haute a hundred miles away with Frederick."

"We'll be all right, Mama!" I shouted, as I dashed out the door behind her and Gus. Our neighbors were coming from all directions. We all headed across town to the fields. I knew the factory workers would leave their work to help. The schools would also close so that the teachers and the older children could help.

"Watch out!" Gus yelled. Mama and I jumped aside as a horse-drawn wagon clattered by. Not the docile animals I was used to seeing at the barns. They were at a full run, their mouths open with hard breathing, their manes and tails whipped about wildly by the wind.

When the field workers had finished husking the corn, they had stacked the ears in big piles at the edge of the field for later hauling. Mama, Gus, and I positioned ourselves by a pile. As a wagon pulled up, we frantically tossed the ears into the wagon and ran to another pile. Other groups were doing the same, shouting directions and encouragement. Most could not be heard above the noise of the wind, the rustle of the corn stalks, and the rattle of the wagons.

My face stung as the wind pelted me with bits of dirt and other debris from the field. Someone ran by and let a corn stalk spring back and strike Gus on the side of the head. He tried to dodge and, off balance, fell against a limb that had been blown from a tree. Seeming to take no notice, he scrambled to right himself and continued the frenzied loading of the wagon.

When each wagon was full, it was rushed to the cribs and another wagon took its place. "Whoa!" shouted the driver. "Jee! Now haw! Now baack! Baack!" he screamed at the horses until he had them lined up close to another pile of corn. White froth lined the leather harness where it came into contact with the horses' heaving sides. Sweat ran down and dripped from their underbellies onto the ground.

Mama used her sleeve to wipe her eyes that stung from perspiration. "Auk, that is all," she said as she threw the last ear into the wagon. Another wagon, partly full of workers, came by and we clambered in and flopped down into the wagon bed. As we raced toward town over dirt roads with paths gouged out by wagon wheel traffic, I was bounced up off the wagon bed and against the side of the wagon each time we hit the bumps.

I was relieved when we got to the cribs and could get out of our wagon to help unload. The last wagon was scarcely unloaded when loud cracks of thunder split the air. Although, I knew that it was still daytime, it looked like night except when jagged streaks of lightning snaked through the sky and for a second brought the daylight back.

As Mama, Gus, and I hurried in through our garden gate, huge drops of rain crashed onto the ground and turned the dust into mud. The wind battered the Lombardy poplars that lined the streets and seemed to threaten the existence of everything in sight.

Inside, I heard Gus breathe a sigh of relief. "We did it. We got the corn in. If we didn't live so close to the cribs, I don't know if I could have made it home," he said breathlessly. He slid down the wall onto the floor and leaned against the door casing.

"Oh, Gus," I said. "You're bleeding."

Mama hurried from the adjoining room. "You're bleeding? Let me see." She gave Gus a close inspection. "It's just a scalp wound. You probably got gouged by that limb. Come with me. I've already washed up. You go next, Emma, while I tend to Gus's wound."

I went to the wash basin, put some soap on a wet flannel cloth and washed my face. I rinsed the cloth in the cold water and used it to wipe away the soap. Then I washed, rinsed, and dried my arms.

"Are you almost finished, Em?" Gus asked.

"Almost," I answered.

I looked at the dirty water. It's still all right for my feet I decided and removed my shoes and stockings. I sat down on a little stool and, with the basin now on the floor, dunked my feet into the water. "Oh, this is wonderful. So soothing to aching, sweaty feet. I could stay here for hours," I murmured. But instead I hurriedly washed and dried my feet and, too tired to eat, drank a glass of cider and went upstairs. But not before I quietly emptied the dirty water and replaced it with clean for Gus.

The fury of the storm subsided and now only gentle rain drops caressed the roof. It sounded delightfully musical. I couldn't wait to snuggle down into my soft cornhusk mattress. And that is just what I did.

Our Harmonie Society had angered our neighbors, the settlers. Mainly over economic and political issues. We owned the only mill, and the settlers claimed that we charged excessive prices to grind their grain. Frederick had bought a tract of land that blocked access to everyone except the Society. So we also controlled shipping. The settlers thought it had been done intentionally. I really don't know.

Since Father Rapp did not speak English well, Frederick who spoke both German and English fluently, handled most of the business that took place in the outside world. Because he understood English, he could better understand the political process. He analyzed all political situations and advised the voters in the Society on how to vote, so the Society voted as one. This meant that things in the county usually went our way. That angered the settlers even more.

They asked for meetings with Frederick and others from the Society in the hopes of coming to some kind of a compromise. Heated debates took place, but in the end they resolved nothing. I remember one day when Frederick went into town and an argument broke out on the street. Frederick was knocked down and kicked when the fracas began.

The settlers had rebelled.

A few days later Frederick began to hear murmurings that they might invade us at the start of the new week. As a precaution, we took refuge in the granary, which actually had been built for the dual purpose of storing grain and also protecting us from the rowdy river pirates who pillaged and plundered. Instead it would protect us from our neighbors.

The intruders did pay a visit. When they were gone, we left the granary only to find that our homes had been vandalized. Those ruffians had swarmed over the entire town. They damaged not only our homes but also the mill, the brewery, the store, a factory, and even Christoph's office.

"Let's go after them," Frederick said quietly. His teeth were clinched and his jaw was set. It took only a few minutes to organize the men, and they filed out of Harmonie.

They were just out of sight when we women realized that we had been duped. The marauding settlers were at our barn rounding up our horses. "Kat, Elsa, Gretchen, all of you! Get anything you can use for weapons and follow me. Get brooms!" I shouted. "Scream, shout, act vicious. Run, don't walk. Put the fear in them. And don't hesitate to swing those weapons!"

The settlers, thinking the men were gone and it was safe to take our horses and livestock, were unprepared. We tore into them–swinging the brooms from whatever end did the most good.

"I got him. I hit him over the head!" shrieked my gentle friend Kat.

"I got one on the knee! He fell to the ground and then got up and ran," Elsa yelled. "I gave him a good limp."

I poked one on the side of his neck with the bristle end of my broom as he ran by. He turned, prepared to fight, but I quickly flipped the broom so the stick end became the weapon. I took a strong stance: feet spaced apart, knees slightly bent, legs braced, both hands on the broom handle which was pointed at this scavenger like a sword. I was stern, unflinching, concentrating with steely eyes on my target. Hate twisted the man's face into a smirk. He stood his ground, but I knew he would have been thought a coward if he hit a woman. He knew it too, and after a moment's hesitation, he spun around and ran after his comrades.

We heard sounds behind us and saw Mama with another group rushing up to join us. They not only had brooms but also skillets and kitchen utensils of every description. I didn't think Mama could do it, but she clobbered a man on his backsides with a skillet that she swung with both hands. It actually lifted him up off the ground a bit. He then went down on his knees and scurried away on all fours.

The enemy had fled. Victory was ours.

We checked the horses, making sure that they were all there. We also made sure that the other animals were unharmed, and secured the barn. Then we began our walk back to our homes. All of us were out of breath, so we stopped at a town pump for water. Only then did we get a good look at one another. Mama had lost her skull cap, and her hair looked a bit like the bristle end of my broom. Kat's apron was nowhere to be seen. Her cap was also gone. Gretchen had fallen and ripped her skirt exposing her pantalets. Only one of my braids was still braided. Bits of straw clung to my hair. I brushed bits of chaff and dirt from my clothes. All of us were dirty, disheveled and a bit bruised. I don't know who lost control first, but uncontrollable laughter broke out releasing all the pent- up energy we had conjured up from some unknown inner source and now no longer needed.

A few days after the "incident" as we called it, I walked to Kat's for a brief visit which, as usual, lasted longer than intended. My skirt swished around my ankles as I hurried toward home. When the clouds floated across the sky and covered the moon, the night went dark. It was then that I heard the footsteps. I moved faster. The footsteps moved faster too.

I was sure one of the rioters, bent on revenge, had returned. I was afraid I was about to be beaten, or worse, killed. Just when I turned around to face my adversary, I was knocked to the ground. A great hairy head hovered over me, breathing foul breath onto my face and bathing it with his slobbers.

"Wolf, get off," I said breathlessly to the huge dog that during the day turned the treadmill for the distillery. I sat on the ground for several seconds trying to regain my composure as he joyously ran in circles and jumped into the air, glad he had found someone to keep him company in the still of the night. I couldn't be angry at Wolf. I was the one out later than I should have been. Anyway, I actually felt safer now that he was trotting along beside me.

I hurried up the garden path, up the steps and opened the door. I had just made it before the nine o'clock curfew. I closed the door as the town crier lit the street lamp outside our house and called:

Again a day is passed, and we are a step nearer our end.
Our time runs out, and the joys of Heaven are our reward.
Nine strokes and all is well.

❧ Winter 1817 ❧

Our first snow of the season had laid a beautiful soft blanket over everything in sight, and it covered the tree limbs with white fluff that sparkled in the sunshine. We were surrounded by an eerie silence, so the sound outside of a horse snorting and harness fittings clattering was startling. Gus went down the hall and opened the door to look out.

"Emma," he said when he came back. "It's John. Do you want to go for a ride in the sleigh?"

"Mama?"

"Yes, Emma. You go. It will be a wonderful drive, like riding through a painting," she answered.

"Gus, tell John it will just take me a minute to get into some warm clothes. I'll hurry."

My heart was pounding. I wondered what encouraged him to extend this invitation. I thought maybe this was a group outing, and he thought it would look strange if I were the only one left out. But from the vantage point I had as I left the house, I could not see anyone else. He was alone.

He helped me into the sleigh. "Here," he said. "Lift your feet." He had warmed some bricks and wrapped them in flannel and slid them under my feet to help keep me warm. He had also brought wool blankets that he spread over our laps. We glided down the street. One of the town pumps covered with snow looked like a funny little man standing guard over the town, the handle that stood straight out looked like an arm pointing directions. As we passed under overhanging branches, snow sifted down upon our heads, attempting to shape us into snow people as we went by.

To fill what was becoming an awkward silence, I asked, "Do you know that the wool in these blankets is probably from our own Merino sheep?"

"I didn't know that. Perhaps you will take me to see the flocks someday soon."

Other people were beginning to venture out, the children laughing as they rolled in the snow and chased each other. Although winter brought some discomfort with it, everyone seemed rejuvenated at the first snow. I thought it might be because the world looked so bright and clean.

John guided the horse around the corner and headed toward the orchards where he stopped and turned to face me. "Emma, what is the situation with you and Aldo Bonn?" he asked.

"I don't know what you mean. There is no situation."

"Well, much of the time when I've seen you, I've seen him with you. I thought..."

"He just shows up. I didn't invite him. I've tried to be polite. But I really don't even like him. That's not exhibiting a kind heart, is it?"

"I don't know about kind hearts, but I do know about happy hearts. That's what I have right now. A very happy heart."

He reached for my hand and held it against his chest over his heart for a moment then slowly slipped each finger out of my glove and kissed each finger tip. I felt strange sensations that I had never felt before, both frightening and wonderful.

"Cricket," he said, "don't you know how I feel about you? I think I fell in love with you the minute I saw you, but you were only fifteen. I wanted to wait. I wanted you to grow up a bit. Then I was afraid I had waited too long. It's been agony for me. Trying to stay out of your way. Then watching Aldo spending time with you..."

A long silence followed. John's dark penetrating eyes held my gaze. "Say something Emma. Am I being a fool? Do you feel nothing for me?"

"John," I began, but my throat tightened and cut off my words.

"I've angered you. I didn't mean to."

"No," I blurted out. "I have longed to hear those words from you for many months. But you seemed to go out of your way to avoid me. I thought you were sending me a message that you had no interest. Now I understand, and I have never known such happiness."

He leaned toward me and my lips willingly met his. I heard his breath catch almost in a gasp. "We need to go, my love," he said abruptly and flicked the horse lightly with the whip.

I sensed that he was right. I too had felt the need to flee, but I also wanted to stay. Even through my confusion, I knew one thing for sure. My life would never be the same from this moment on.

✦ Winter 1818 ✦

"Mama, I'll sleep in the common room and tend the fire tonight," I said.

"Just make sure that by morning we have only red coals. Not fire, just live coals," Mama said.

I could almost hear a smile in her voice. I knew she was remembering the first time I had been trusted to keep the fire going throughout the night. So afraid I would let the fire die, I kept stoking it until I had the house too warm. We had to throw open the door and all the windows so the freezing outside air could rush in and cool us down to a comfortable level again.

After that episode Papa gave me a detailed description of the construction of our house. Being master craftsmen, our men folk had long ago devised a way to keep our houses warm in the winter and cool in the summer.

Dutch biscuits, eighteen inch boards wrapped in straw and mud, were installed in the ceiling and soft bricks were placed inside the walls. That made wonderful insulation for both summer and winter. The unusual chimney also had much to do with the success of our winter comfort. On the first floor the large chimney provided a cooking fireplace, but it was also vented into the common room as a heat source. Then it went up through the ceiling and provided fireplaces for the bedrooms above.

"Now you know you don't have to heat the outside world," Papa joked. "The builders planned our comfort well. We just need to help things along a little. No harm done. A lesson learned," he added.

The kinder Papa was when I made mistakes, the worse I felt. It had always been that way between Papa and me.

Gus had cleared a narrow path through the snow to our barn so he could tend the cows and chickens. We not only had a community barn but also a small one close to the house. The small one was divided into two parts: one part housed a cow and a few chickens, the other part was a privy. Gus finished the feeding and hurried back to the warmth of the house. As he hung his coat on the peg just inside the door, he announced, "I have outgrown my boots again, Papa. They are making my feet hurt."

"I can fix that," Papa said and shortly came in with a paper. "Stand here and put your foot on this paper," he said. "Let's get you measured." Then as Gus set his foot down on the paper, Papa made a notch for the length of the foot and one for the width. "I will take this measurement to the cobbler tomorrow so new boots can be made for you. When I pick up your new ones, I will leave these. You outgrow them so fast you leave much good in them. I'm sure some other boy, maybe one of the immigrants, will be pleased to have them."

"I have been forgetting to mention that we know why the immigrants we were expecting had not arrived yet," he added. "Both groups got a late start. One group encountered bad weather in Dover, England. They lost the mast on their ship and the rudder broke, so they will not be here until spring. The other group was shipwrecked in Norway, but no one was seriously hurt."

"We wouldn't have had much work for them until spring anyway," Mama replied. "But I'm glad they're safe and being cared for in the meantime. Emma, tomorrow we will catch up on mending. Maybe later the snow will be cleared enough so we can get over to Dormitory 2 for some singing."

"Do I have to go?" Gus asked.

"Gus, you are not a good German if you don't like singing," Papa teased.

"I like singing. I just can't sing," Gus answered.

"I want you to go with the family. You can listen," Papa said. "I'm going up to bed. Good night." He turned and looked at Mama. "Good night, Gerta," he said.

I had seen that look before. I had felt it. That look that passed between Mama and Papa sometimes.

"Don't read too long and be sure to put out the flame on the lamp," Mama told me as she picked up a candle in its holder and went toward the stairs.

Since our dwelling housed only our own family, we had taken the liberty to organize according to our own needs. Usually the men slept upstairs and the women slept down, but we revised that. Papa and Gus slept in one bedroom upstairs, and Mama and I slept in the other across the hall except when one of us needed to be in the common room to tend the fire.

I answered Mama with a slight smile, remembering once when she got up in the middle of the night and thought she saw a light flickering in the hall. Tracing its origin, she discovered that it was coming from the common room downstairs where I had been tending the night fire. I had been reading as usual and had gone to sleep with the lamp still burning. I was using our Betty lamp, an iron container filled with fat drippings and fitted with a wick of twisted cloth. It had a handle-like appendage with a hole in the end so it could be hung on the wall or it could be carried or placed on a table. Long ago Papa told me that the word *Betty* came from the German word *bete*, which meant better. And it did give much better light than candles. I could read much longer without my eyes stinging.

I checked the fire in the pot-bellied iron stove one last time before I went to bed. I reminded myself to tell Papa that the ropes needed to be tightened on the common room bed. Neither I, nor anyone else, could get a sound sleep with the sagging support that held the corn husk mattress.

Papa was concerned about the Society's ability to supply our usual customers. Winter had indeed made itself known this year by barging in early and unannounced. The Society needed to ship products in small boats because of the possibility that the river would soon freeze over. John Baker wrote that he had sold all the flour in Shawneetown, Illinois, and the store owner there was worried that he would be short of everything for Christmas. His customers were already inquiring. Baker also wanted the entire stock of jeans we had because that was what attracted his customers. Our jeans were the best quality for miles around. We had word from Vincennes that they needed several pounds of coarse woolen yarn suitable for making carpets. Drs. McNarnee and Shuler liked the white wine and would recommend it to their patients if we could get it to them.

With all that on Papa's mind, there was more to come. Gus had run to the house shouting, "Papa, come quick. Our cow gave birth, but I think the calf is dead. I think it froze to death."

Papa yanked on his boots and put on his coat as he ran out, and I ran after him.

"The calf has some warmth in its body," Papa said. He lifted it off the ground by its hind legs and hit it hard on the chest with the flat of his hand then waited. Nothing. He hit it again. Still no response. He turned it around and hit it on the other side. This time the calf began to breathe. "Emma, get some wool blankets from the house. Hurry!" he said.

When I returned Papa told me, "It's too late. The calf quit breathing again, and I couldn't bring him back."

"Papa, I hurried as fast as I could."

"That wasn't it, Emma. He had been cold too long, and it was too early for him to be born. He didn't have the strength to suckle and get warm milk into his belly."

"It's a real loss, isn't it Papa?" Gus asked.

"Yes, we could have sold this calf and put the money in the Society's savings for our trip to Jerusalem. We certainly want to get there in time for the Second Coming. Nothing more I can do here," he said as he picked up the tiny calf and took it away as he left.

When I was little, I would have wanted to sing hymns and have prayers for that little animal. A few times when Father Rapp passed by during one of my ceremonies, he had graciously said a prayer for the departed, no matter what it was. Once, it was just for a little naked baby bird that had fallen from its nest. He thanked Vater Gott for creating wonderful creatures such as the little song bird and said our hearts were heavy because it would never sing. He said we were happy that the other little birds in the nest would sing more often and louder to make up for the loss.

I started to leave the barn, but Gus stopped me with his questions. "Emma, do you think the Lord really will return soon? Do you think that we will ever really go to Jerusalem?" he asked.

"You mustn't go by what I believe, Gus. Father Rapp says we must listen closely to the Word and that eventually we will understand and can make our own decisions about what to believe."

"I will, Em. But tell me what you believe."

"No, Gus. The Society is our own little world of freedom. We are free to make our own choices. When we come of age, we are even free to leave here if we choose. All your decisions and mine must be our own. They cannot be made by anyone else."

"Will you do that, Em?"

"What?"

"Leave here."

"Gus, please don't ask me any more questions. Ask Papa or Mama. Or ask Father Rapp." I already knew that if John asked me to go to the end of the earth with him, I would go.

❧ Autumn 1819 ❧

Gus was excited. He was going fox hunting with the brothers. They never hunt alone but always in large groups. For fox hunting, the men and boys would form a long line horizontal to the river and slowly walk in that direction. Any foxes that were present on the prairie would be driven slowly toward the shooters who were secluded at the tree line. Gus explained to me how the drivers circled around to get out of the line of fire. I still don't know exactly how it worked, but as long as the men did and were safe, I guess that's one good thing about the whole procedure.

"I don't know how you can harm those beautiful little creatures Gus," I told him.

"The hides are bringing a good price right now."

"Well, I don't like to think about it." And I tried not to for the rest of the day. And when I heard the men returning, even though it was quite cold, I went for a long walk so I wouldn't have to see those little animals carried in by their tails with their heads flopping about.

Trouble was brewing in our little world. We had developed economic trouble. Frederick believed part of the problem was that people thought manufactured goods purchased from abroad were better than those made locally. So when they could, they bought things from other countries. He criticized the government for not enacting protective tariffs. Because the Society was mostly self-sufficient, we were not affected as much as others by the depression that was brewing. Although we were somewhat balanced among manufacturing and commerce, we were rooted in agriculture, so we always had plenty of good food to eat. But more and more, the workshops had less and less work.

Currency was unstable and banks were drowning in fraud and corruption. The bank in Vincennes finally failed, even though Frederick tried his best to save it. Eventually Harmonie established its own bank. It was kept free from corruption and political interference with Frederick as the president and John Baker as cashier.

It wasn't long before I heard rumors about going back to Pennsylvania. Those rumors struck fear in my heart. If the rumors were true, what would John do? Would he go to Pennsylvania or would he stay here? Or would he leave for an unknown destination? I wondered if there was anything else besides economic trouble that was causing the unrest. Surely there was more.

When I got home, Papa was cleaning his boots and Mama was mending, which seemed to be what we women did in spare moments.

"Papa, I stopped by Solomon's to see how that injured mare was getting along. She's much better and going to be good as new according to Solomon."

"There is no one like Solomon when it comes to healing our animals," Papa interrupted.

Mama smiled. "And sometimes our people," she added.

"He mentioned that we might go back to Pennsylvania. We won't, will we?"

"There is some talk, Emma, but right now it is only talk. I will say, however, that everything has not gone as expected since we came here."

"What, Papa? Only the slow markets? I heard you say the markets would eventually recover, so that shouldn't be a big problem, should it?"

"There's more, Emma. The people in Pennsylvania are used to Germans, so they are more tolerant of us and our way of life. Back there we would have fewer conflicts because there would be better understanding. If a conflict between Harmonists and locals goes to court here, the judge usually favors the local villagers."

"Also, Emma," Mama said, "The climate here will always threaten us with malaria. We have lost many good people to that scourge."

"I heard Frederick talking about the East Coast markets being too far away for us now," Gus added, "and about the postal service being much too slow and undependable. He thinks that by moving, some of those problems will be solved."

"It's still just talk, Emma," Mama said.

I nodded. I did understand. But my heart was heavy.

❖ Spring 1820 ❖

Spring arrived demanding our full attention as usual. Some of the men white washed the insides of the frame houses and dorms to protect the wood from termites. They scrubbed the floors with sand, swept them clean, then washed them with lye soap and water. After they were rinsed well, they would dry almost white. Some of the men hauled rocks and others cleared brush. Another group pushed the greenhouses away from the fruit trees.

When Father Rapp found that the climate in southwestern Indiana was not as warm as he had thought, he devised a plan for protecting the citrus trees that had already been planted. He had the men build long houses on wheels so they could roll them over the seedlings before winter. Now it was time to roll them away so the trees could soak up the warm sun.

We cleaned the soot out of our stove pipes, removed remnants of ashes from the fireplaces, and gave a good scrubbing to the stone sink and to the drain that went out through the wall to the barrel outside.

Everyday work continued also. Gus fed the chickens and collected the eggs. Papa milked the cow so it would be ready to go to the community pasture when the herdsman came. He saved the allotted pint of milk per person and put the rest out to be picked up by the community milk wagon. At the dairy, it would be made into butter and cheese. Since there was no milk and no eggs during the winter, having both again in the spring was a real treat.

Each day brought more of the same, but as it turned out for us, one day was different. Gus would be sixteen years old today, and although all of us were aware of it, it would be amiss to draw attention to it. We did not want to imply that he was more important than other boys in the Society.

Mama hummed softly as she started her preparations for lunch. Before long wonderful fragrances filled the house. I offered to help, but Mama kindly refused, so I continued the mending I had started the day before. As I pushed my needle in and out of the hem on my other skirt as I had done many times before, I remembered being told about Father Rapp having to have two old German coats pieced together into one when we first arrived in America.

Mama announced that our lunch was ready and let me help her carry the sumptuous meal to the table. There was homemade bread and our own butter brought up from the crock in the cellar. Beyond that we had veal and rice stew, spiced peaches, applesauce cake and cider.

"Would it be verboten for me to say the prayer today, Yurgen?" she asked.

"I guess it could be held acceptable once," he replied.

"Vater Gott," Mama said, "thank you for blessing us now and also sixteen years ago today. Amen."

I glanced at Papa. He seemed preoccupied with watching the little stove in the common room as if waiting for it to come to life and voice some objections. Gus gazed intently at his plate. Mama had startled us by slipping in more than a hint about Gus's birthday. She even had reminded Vater Gott. Was Papa angry, I wondered? I could not tell since I could not see his face. My thoughts were reeling. I had never seen any trouble between Mama and Papa. What if today would be the day? I drowned my thoughts by tracing the wood grain patterns in the tabletop.

Mama always acknowledged our birthdays but subtly. She always made a special dish or baked a special treat or put beautiful flowers on the table. When I got old enough to have a bit of discernment, I noticed and eventually pointed it out to Gus but cautioned him to keep it our secret. I did not think Papa ever was aware.

I knew one thing for certain. I had a wonderfully warm feeling in my soul that day. Papa said nothing at all, but on the way out as he passed Mama, I saw him briefly touch her shoulder. I am sure Papa wanted to let Gus know how pleased he was to have him born into our family, but he just didn't know how. The rest of the day Gus was particularly helpful to Mama, and his love for her shone in his eyes. I was sorry to have that day end.

How strange are some of our ways. To those outside our house, Gus may not have been more important than anyone else within the Society, but to Mama and Papa and me, he was part of our world. We wouldn't have known what to do without him. How can we deny that? And why should we have to?

———————

We were still aglow with thoughts of yesterday, but it did not take long for that to be pushed aside so we could concentrate on today. Getting the corn planted was an important part of spring. Boys placed poles every four and a half feet as a guide for the man with the horse-drawn plow, which then was pulled across the field cutting furrows according to the markers. The next day the furrows were cut four and a half feet apart horizontal to the originals. That method formed squares into which workers dropped four or five grains of corn from a basket they carried on their arm. Others followed behind and dropped two or three pumpkin seeds in every third square, and the next group came along with hoes to cover the seeds.

One day Frederick stopped by with a visitor to see how things were going. They both removed their jackets and helped with the work. Late in the afternoon everyone sat down under shade trees and had bread, butter, cheese and cider and enjoyed a few songs. Then work continued until sundown, but when the day was done the work had seemed almost like pleasure because of the camaraderie.

Mama and Papa helped that day as did Sophie and Thorben Schaefer, Kat's parents, and many others. John and I managed to sit by each other when we had our *vesper brodt*, and we managed to select a small tree slightly apart from the group. Although it was not verboten for an unmarried couple to be friends, they usually stayed in a group. It was not the normal thing for a couple to pair off as John and I were doing, and I was still trying to sort things out in my mind.

"I think they're watching us," I told him.

"I think you might be right, but I am wondering if that is a bad thing. We have to handle this, Cricket. There is nothing wrong with our love. Let's not make it seem so."

"I know you're right. I'll talk to Mama. Just give me time to plan what I want to say."

"What do you want to say, Em? I'm interested in hearing that myself."

"I want to say that I love you. I want to say that I love you more than life itself. That I wonder if I could ever manage to live without you."

I knew that all the love in my heart shone through my eyes for all to see when I turned to look at him. How could people not know? Why had I been finding it so hard to let the words find their way out into the open?

"Emma, do you know how hard it is for me at this moment to sit here and refrain from gathering you up into my arms to hold you close to my heart? I'm going to move away now. I have to. You handle this your own way, my love."

John joined a group that was listening to a chorus of singers. He leaned against a tree then turned to look back. I saw his eyes. They were filled with love. Like Papa's eyes sometimes when he looked at Mama and hers when she looked at him. How had I missed that all these years? They loved each other, really loved each other. They were not like most couples in the Society, those who were quite content to live as brother and sister because their union was an arrangement that had nothing to do with love. I hadn't really thought much about it, but most of those couples seemed to like and respect each other. It was just that no love showed when they looked at each other. Perhaps Mama and Papa's union had been an arrangement also, but if so, it had grown into real love.

"I'm glad it's a cloudy day today," I told Mama. "I would not like staying inside to do all this mending if it were a pleasant sunshiny day."

"Doing the kind of work we do in the spring means that every time we look around something else has been torn and must be repaired," Mama replied.

I waited for her to say more, but she didn't. In the silence my mind raced about untethered. There were so many things I didn't understand. I'm sure Mama and Papa were chosen for each other by their parents. They obviously learned to love each other after they were married. Maybe

the love that John and I have for each other before marriage is unusual, maybe suspicious, maybe unacceptable.
Why else would I have had such an obsession about keeping it a secret? Maybe the secrecy is that which is making
me feel guilty.

"Mama," I said.

I waited. My eyes were downcast, but I knew she was
looking at me. Still she said nothing. When I finally looked
at her, my words tumbled out end over end. "I love John,
Mama. I want to marry him some day."

"I know."

"You know? How did you know?" I asked.

"I saw your eyes when you looked at him. And I saw
his eyes when you were with him. The soul is in the eyes
and good or bad, what is there cannot be hidden."

"I don't know what to tell Papa," I said.

"He already knows," Mama said.

"He knows too? And what did he say?" I asked.

"He likes John and, as I do, thinks he is a good man. He
wishes things would have been a bit different. He's afraid
that John might leave and you would go with him. That
wouldn't happen if you had chosen someone in the Society. And we don't believe in coercing people to join us.
That includes John."

"I know that, Mama. Should I talk to Papa even if he
knows already about John and me?"

"I think he would feel terrible if you didn't. And then
tell Gus. He loves you too and wants you to be happy.
And he also is afraid you might leave. We really don't know
much about John's background. We don't even know where
he lived before he came here."

"I mentioned it once, and he said we would talk about
it some day, and I never asked again. Gus knows too?
About John and me?" I asked.

"As do many others," Mama said.

"I thought only Kat knew. Did she tell people? I'm going to be so disappointed if she has given away my secret."

"You aren't listening carefully. It hasn't been a secret for quite some time. And Kat told no one. Your eyes and John's revealed the secret."

"I've been cowardly, Mama. And foolish."

"None of us is perfect and all of us are foolish from time to time," Mama answered. "Remember the labyrinth. There are no dead ends and if we take a wrong turn, we can circle back and try again. Eventually we find our way."

❧ Autumn 1821 ❧

One day I suggested to John that we go for a walk, and he wanted to walk over to the labyrinth south of town. "I've walked by it many times," he said, "but I'm still not sure I know what its purpose is. It's like a maze, isn't it?"

"Sort of, but then it differs in some ways. I think a maze is usually in the shape of a square or rectangle with many zigzag pathways. It has an entrance on one side and an exit on the other with many dead ends that block your way and force you to go back and try a different path. The object is to find your way to the exit. A labyrinth is circular, at least both of ours have been, and its entrance and exit are the same. It also has zigzag pathways but no dead ends. Ours are outside and are formed by having tall shrubs on each side of the paths. You go round and round trying to find your way. After many trials and errors, you finally find a little temple in the center. The outside of the little building is rough and not at all attractive. There is a door with no handle, and it blends in with the rest of the structure so you have to feel around and push here and there searching for it. Journeying through a labyrinth is rather like trying to find the meaning of life. It is well-hidden but when you finally do get inside, you see a place of beauty and you find a feeling of peace. Father Rapp says a labyrinth is symbolic, a sermon all by itself."

"Let's start down one of these paths and see what happens," John said when we arrived at the labyrinth. "I want to see if I can find the beauty that waits in the center for those who persevere. Oh, just a minute. I will search only for the peace that is promised. I already have the beauty right here by my side. Do you want to lead the way?"

"You are going to ruin me, and I will have to leave the Society," I teased. "You know we don't dwell on outward appearances."

"I do know that, but I really like looking at the outward appearance," John replied with a smile and a twinkle in his eyes.

I thought it best to change the subject so I told him, "As we find our way through here, I will tell you about getting lost in the labyrinth in Pennsylvania when I was a little girl. Then you may not want me to lead the way."

"I always want to hear about your life. Being lost in a labyrinth sounds like a real adventure. Were you afraid? How old were you?"

Before I could answer, I heard Gus calling. We had just started down a path.

"In here, Gus. Follow the sound of my voice."

"Sorry, Em. Mama sent me," he said when he caught up to us.

"I thought she probably would. It's all right. You can help us find the temple."

"Actually, Mama wanted you to know that Gertrude and her quartet are going to be singing shortly and the orchestra will be playing. She wanted you to come right away so you could hear them."

"Of course. We'll go with you," I said, and we turned around and headed back.

Mama was subtle and clever. Well, clever anyway. She knew quite well that Gertrude, as talented as she was, would not entice me back under the circumstances. But my mama's voice would, even from a distance.

Gertrude was Father Rapp's granddaughter and had lived with him and his wife Christina, since her father was killed in a mill accident in Pennsylvania a few years prior. Mama said Gertrude was nothing short of a miracle because she was given everything she wanted and more, yet she still remained humble and kind. Because we had a good school in Pennsylvania and another good one here in Harmonie, most of us in the younger generation were fairly well educated. But about three years ago, Gertrude went away for more education. For one thing, she studied advanced English classes in the Shaker settlement near Vincennes. Gertrude was already a skilled artist and loved to paint wildlife, especially her pet elk that had been found orphaned some time ago. She was also a trained vocalist and musician.

I was not able to take advantage of such a luxury as studying anywhere but in Harmonie. I continued to study in our library that housed hundreds of books, and I had no trouble finding tutors delighted to help me. Several in the Society composed music worthy of publishing, and many were students of literature, art and science. "I have a strange sister," Gus used to say. "She loves to study."

"You come too, John," I said. "You will want to hear the music, I know."

"Yes," John said, "I was hoping we could do that today."

Gus turned quickly and looked at us to see if we were joking or angry. We somehow managed to keep our faces sober as we continued our stroll toward town. We truly did enjoy music, but we would have preferred to be by ourselves to develop our special friendship.

Gus stopped and faced us. "You really don't want to go back to town to listen to music, do you?"

"No!" we shouted in unison.

We were all smiling by then, and levity saved the situation. Hopefully, it kept me from becoming sullen, which I was inclined to do when I was younger. I would never talk back to Mama or Papa, but when I was angry, my not talking at all or talking in monosyllables left nothing to the imagination. I was always sorry later for my behavior. Sometimes Mama would say quietly, "That's enough, Emma. Go for a walk and come back with a different face."

The music was beautiful I must admit, but frequently during the performance, I envisioned John and me still at the labyrinth.

❧ Summer 1822 ❧

My little world seemed to be falling apart. The markets still had not improved, and Father Rapp and Frederick were at odds. Not at odds about the problems with the economy but about Father Rapp and his assistant, Hildegard Mutschler, a bright, attractive young woman whose behavior was unseemly. She had become quite friendly with one man, and Father expelled the man from the Society and asked the congregation to pray for Hildegard. When the man left the Society, some members, who considered the expulsion unjust, left also. When Hildegard fell in love with another and left the Society with him, Father was annoyed with anyone who spoke against her. Instead he asked the congregation to pray for her return, and he didn't expel her as he would have done to anyone else. I wondered if John had heard the talk and what he thought about it. That question was answered when he once told me that we had elevated our leader high above his position.

Our community became involved in a big building project. Three times Father Rapp had a vision of a church that was in the shape of a Maltese cross, and he wanted to have it built. It would be brick and would insulate us from the dreadfully hot summers and the cold winters. Everyone was excited when the building started, and we followed its progress with great interest. I thought this came at a good time because it gave us something to think about besides Hildegard Mutschler and the economy.

In August we had our Erntefest, our yearly harvest festival. We had thick rice soup, roast veal and roast beef fixed together, sauerkraut, ginger cakes, and wine. There was preaching, singing, music by our orchestra, and wonderful camaraderie. It would only be another month before the leaves of the sassafras would turn a rich, bright orange then brilliant red. It was a signal that autumn was on its way, winter was not far behind, and another year would be gone forever.

My thoughts were interrupted by someone asking for Gus. "Who was that?" I asked Mama.

"One of the brothers that I don't know," she replied. "Gus is needed to help hitch the oxen to a Noah's ark."

I remembered when John saw a Noah's ark for the first time. "What is that?" he had asked me.

"The herdsmen stay with the sheep in the meadows day and night. They have to have shelter, so the brothers designed and built long houses on wheels for that purpose and called them Noah's arks. They have to be pulled to location by oxen," I had told him.

I was glad when I saw Gus return. "It's good that everything went well. It seems to me that many things have gone wrong this year. If anything else is going to go wrong," I told him, "I hope it will just get it over with." And in answer to my comment, two of the cobbler's apprentices ran away.

"*Abgewichen*. Two of the boys," Papa said.

I turned toward John who had just come in and said, "Gone astray. That's what *abgewichen* means."

John acknowledged the interpretation and asked, "What will the cobbler do?"

"He has already searched for Ludwig and could not find him. He is tired out and no longer cares about him or the other one either. They both probably will be back. Life is harder out there than they realize," Papa answered.

"They have it so good here," Mama agreed. "I never understand why anyone wants to leave."

"Ludwig was there when I went with Gus to pick up his boots," I said. "He seemed like such a nice boy, friendly and happy. He was water proofing the boots and took time to show me how to rub the mixture of drying oil, burgundy pitch, turpentine and... What else, Gus?"

"Spirits of yellow wax, I think," he responded.

"Yes, that's it. And now he has run away. It is so easy to be deceived. From one day to the next, we do not know what will come about."

❖ Spring 1823 ❖

Kat and I took a brief moment to sit on the bench in their garden among the flowers. Pink, white, lavender and blue sweet peas were waving gently in the breeze, their tendrils attached to a fence her papa had made. The blossoms reminded me of butterflies, and it seemed that their fragrance permeated the whole block. Such restful places, our gardens. Our plan was to go down by the river where Father Rapp and others were gathering to see a steamboat, the first one to come up the Wabash. We saw Will with Thorben and Sofie, Kat's parents, leaving.

"Come along shortly," Sofie called.

We both waved to let her know that we heard.

"We are lucky to be living in Harmonie in our Society," I told Kat. "We have every right to feel safe and secure here. We are even better off than the State of Indiana. Samuel Merrill, the State Treasurer, wrote to Frederick and asked if the Society could loan Indiana five thousand dollars. I believe that Frederick replied in the affirmative. I guess the state is broke. Can you imagine an entire state being broke?"

It was a rhetorical question not requiring an answer, so I rambled on. "I am sorry for Christoph. He must be humiliated to have a brother like Eugen."

"What happened this time?" Kat asked.

"Well, Eugen knows that it is our custom only to drink wine or beer or cider. But he is a breaker of rules and his mind is frequently befuddled with whiskey. That's why the soap he makes falls apart much of the time. This last episode was worse. He left the soap factory with no one there to oversee it and went to get his whiskey. The soap boiled over and ran out into the street. Then..."

"What was that loud noise?" Kat interrupted. Simultaneously with the noise, birds flew from the trees in frightened flocks, the ground shook, and smoke could be seen in the distance.

We ran toward the screams and shouts. As we got closer we saw people running here and there in total confusion. Gretchen called to me and I paused momentarily to tell her that I didn't yet know what was happening. Kat ran on ahead. It was shortly thereafter that I heard what sounded like an animal in dreadful pain. Then an ear-piercing scream that seemed to have no end cut through the smoke.

I heard John call to me. As I turned I saw him hurrying toward me. "Don't go there, Em. Please!" he said.

But I seemed to be drawn toward the river and the people, and I didn't know how to stop. I pressed on. I saw Kat on the ground cradling Will in her arms. It was she who was making the strange sounds that I didn't recognize. I hardly recognized her face as it was contorted in agony. She was calling hysterically for Christoph.

Sofie was stretched out on the ground across the way and Thorben was rubbing her arms and patting her cheeks. She slowly sat up and he helped her to her feet.

I hurried to Kat in what seemed like slow motion. I knew I was hurrying, but I seemed to be making no headway. Christoph was trying to take Will from Kat's embrace. Blood covered Will's face and soaked his shirtwaist.

"Help him, Christoph," she begged.

"It's too late, Katerina," Christoph said. "It's too late. Will has gone to be with God. Let him go."

"Not yet, Christoph. Please, not yet." She tightened her grip and gathered Will closer to her chest.

Sophie moved slowly. She knelt down by Kat and moved Will away a bit. "Let your papa take him, Kat," she said gently. Kat's eyes were empty when she glanced at her mother. She nodded vaguely as Thorben and Christoph took Will from her.

They carried Will away and Sophie sat down on the ground beside Kat. As Kat laid her head against her mother's shoulder, Sofie began to rock her back and forth and to hum softly as one would do for an infant.

I turned away.

———•———

Gus. Where was Gus? And Mama and Papa? Where were they?

At the exact moment of my thoughts, John and Gus appeared. Gus had a blood-soaked bandage that John had applied to the left arm just below the elbow. Christoph's training had come in handy that day. John had learned well and was a great help in the crisis.

"Mama and Papa are fine, Em," Gus told me. "They are both helping the injured. You are looking at my bandage. It's only a minor wound."

"I'm glad." I said. "What happened here?"

"Father Rapp wanted to welcome the first steamboat that was coming down the Wabash, so he appointed a group of men to fire the cannon, but by mistake they overloaded it and it exploded. One man lost a foot, another was seriously injured, several others had minor injuries, but no one was killed."

"Will..."

"What, Em? What about Will?" Gus asked.

"He...he was...he was killed," I said in a whisper because I no longer had the strength to speak otherwise. I leaned against the trunk of the sugar maple then slid slowly down and melted into a heap. Gus sat down beside me.

"How? What happened?" he asked.

"I don't know. He was covered in blood."

"Em," he said, "we do not have to wonder about Will's place in eternity. We do not fear death."

"I know," I answered. "It isn't that. It's that I already miss him. And I ache for Kat, Sofie and Thorben. They will miss him even more. One of these days I'll remember Will, not with this dreadful ache in my heart, but with a smile for all the pleasure he brought us. I'm sure of it. But I can't do it right now."

Gus stood and extended a hand to help me up. He pointed to Mama who was walking toward us. Then he went back to help the many others who were still there doing what they could to restore order.

"Mama!" I exclaimed. "I could not find you or Papa. I saw Gus and he told me you both were all right. What can I do to help?"

"I heard about Will, Emma. I'm so sorry. I loved him too." She laid her hand on my arm and looked into my eyes as if intending to say something more but instead she said, "I think Christoph could use some help at the hospital."

I walked back to town and into the hospital where I was greeted with much appreciation by Christoph. First on my list of duties was to get the patients cleaned up. Then I helped John apply bandages, I gave medicines and treatments as Christoph instructed, and I held the hands of those in distress. I worked long and hard and was numb from exhaustion when I got home.

Sometimes one of life's greatest blessings is to be numb from exhaustion.

———·+·——

Will's body was kept at home for three days in a plain hexagonal coffin like the ones used for everyone else whose life spirit had left. After three days, the family and invited friends followed the coffin to the departed's temporary repose by the orchard in *Gottsacker* or as we say in English, God's Acre. Temporary, because as Father Rapp quoted from the book of Corinthians:

"In a moment, in a twinkling of an eye, the dead shall be raised."

That was all I remembered about Father Rapp's comments. I was instead watching as the soft rays of the late evening sun splashed across the clouds turning the sky gold. Evening deepened quickly. A gentle breeze played with the clouds, nudging them apart to let the sun shine down on us briefly before moving aside to let the clouds drift back together and obscure the sun. Toying with us. Rather like life. Days with sunshine and days with clouds.

I clung tightly to John's hand as images of Will raced through my mind: Will kissing the frog, Will imitating a bunny rabbit, Will stained blue from berry picking. I could still see him standing in the doorway calling to Kat and me. "Where are you going? I want to go with you."

I hoped his spirit was still close enough to hear me silently tell him, "You will go with me. Always. In my heart and in my memory."

For me, the year after Will's death was bathed in a misty fog. Sometimes I fought anger and at other times sadness when I saw that the Society seemed to be operating as it always had, as if they did not remember that Will had once been alive and living among us and now was gone. I myself, felt guilty for feeling pleasure in John's presence. Childlike, I wanted to tell God that I didn't want Will to be up there anymore, that I was ready for him to come back now. Time inched by, and eventually my life returned to a close facsimile of the normal life I once had known.

✢ Winter 1824 ✢

In January a law had been passed to move the seat of government from Corydon to Indianapolis. Frederick had been actively involved in getting that done. He was a man of many abilities, and we had been lucky to have him with us. John, however, said that Frederick was not without fault as I seemed to think. He said when our neighbors complained about anything at all, Frederick was prone to accuse them of fighting against the cause of Jesus. The neighbors said Jesus had nothing to do with it. They just wanted their rights. It seemed to me that the world which once appeared so simple was fast becoming more complex.

I heard my name and looked up to see John walking toward me. "I know it is serious when you call me Emma," I told him with a smile.

"It is serious."

"Should I sit down to receive this serious announcement?"

"Let's walk down to the orchard where there's a bench."

"I really do need to sit?"

"I think you probably will."

We walked in silence. My lightheartedness had totally disappeared, and, for some unknown reason, my heart was filled with foreboding. I glanced at John. His face was grim. When we got to the orchard, I saw that Frederick had placed vases filled with little red star flowers on the tables. If flowers were supposed to lift the spirits, right now it wasn't working.

Finally John broke the silence. "I have a story to tell you, Emma. Please don't interrupt. Just wait until I've finished. Will you do that for me? It's important."

I could only nod.

"My given name is Giovanni Donato. My heritage is Italian. You know that. You have rules to follow here in Harmonie, and I also had rules to follow in my family but ones very different. My parents chose a wife for me. That was the way it was done there. The two sets of parents got together and decided that I would make a good husband for Madalena and that she would make a good wife for me. We, neither of us, had any say in the matter. We scarcely knew each other. I could not go through with the marriage, so I ran away before it became an issue. I am sure my parents felt disgraced.

I have three things I need to do. I need to make amends with my parents. Then I need to release Madalena from her promise. Also, I have some inheritance waiting for me. It is some money that my grandfather left me. I want to sign the papers or whatever needs to be done. I want to marry you, Emma. It is you that I love, and I don't want to come to you empty-handed."

We sat for a long time in silence. "Say something, Em."

"Don't go. Please don't go. By now this Madda person probably has married someone else. And I don't want the money. You know that money is not important to me."

"It's something I have to do, Em. It has to do with honor. But the story goes from honor to shame, Em. I have not been in touch with my parents since I left. I was afraid they would send someone to take me home if they knew where I was. Then weeks melted into months and months into years. It's possible that they think I am dead."

"It must be terrible for them. Wondering about you."

"Yes, I'm sure it is, and I want above all else to set that right. Now about us. You're sure you love me? If you are, could we say our vows to each other before I leave? I want there to be something that binds us. Then when I get back, we will have a real wedding. One with Father Rapp offici-ating if you like. Say that you love me."

"I think I've loved you since I first saw you. You and your dark wavy hair and dark eyes. How striking you looked! Then the more I got to know you, it was not just the way you looked. It was the way you were living your life: working so hard, helping anyone who needed help. I began to care for you more and more. Sometimes I won-dered what I would do if you did not some day learn to love me back."

"I always loved you back. You just didn't know it."

"But you didn't know that I loved you and had for a long time. Life is cruel sometimes, keeping secrets that should not be kept."

"But maybe the secret was revealed at the proper time. I guess we will never know. It is enough to know that I love you and you love me," he smiled. "Meet me tomor-row, Emma. Can you come in the afternoon after *vesper brodt* so we can say our vows? There will be a boat coming in next week and..."

"Nooo! Not so soon! Please, John. Not so soon."

"I planned it this way, Em. It will be easier for both of us if it's quick. And the sooner I leave, the sooner I will return."

"I'm going for a walk," I told Mama. "I may stop for Kat, but no matter what, I'll be back in time to help with supper."

Mama glanced up briefly and nodded. "Put on your cloak. The air still has a chill in it."

John was at the barn as planned and I told him, "I'm sorry. This is so important, but I must hurry, I don't have much time."

"I know," he answered as he took both my hands in his and kissed me on the forehead. "I'll go first."

Emma, from this day on, you shall not walk alone. I will be with you whether near or far. I will love you with my every breath for all my life and beyond.

"Now you, Emma."

John, from this day on, I give you my loyalty and my heart. You are a part of my hopes and dreams. You are my friend and my love completely and forever.

"March 3, 1824. This is the anniversary I will remember, the real one. When we have the other ceremony, it will just be play-acting. Now may I kiss the bride, Mrs. Giovanni Donato?"

Papa turned around to see who was coming in. "Emma, what... What happened to you?"

"I slipped and fell. It's my ankle, Papa. The pain sent me to the stream down by the river to put it in cold water. I'm sorry to be so late."

"But your skull cap is off, and...here, Emma. You've been crying. Are you still in pain? Do you want me to go for Christoph?"

"No, Papa. I don't need Christoph, but could I please be excused from supper this evening? I want to lie down."

"Of course. I'll send Gus up with a glass of cider and some ginger cookies. In the morning if the injury is not better, I'll send for Christoph."

"Thank you, Papa."

It was Mama who brought the cider and ginger cookies. "If you need to take your shoe off and soak your foot some more, I brought a pitcher of cold water." Mama was silent for a moment. "Do you need to...do you need...anything?"

"No thank you, Mama," I said. "I just want to rest." And I turned my face to the wall and listened to Mama's footsteps going slowly down the stairs and disappearing into the common room.

"Emma, let us walk. To our favorite place, the orchard perhaps? Is your ankle able?"

"Yes, Mama. That would be nice. My ankle doesn't bother me today."

We found a bench. I knew Mama brought me here to ask questions. I thought about this all night. Sometimes Mama seems to see into my mind, and I think this is one of those times. Things were muddled enough. I dare not muddle it more by lies, so I plunged in.

"Mama, John is leaving. He has to go to Italy for some business. He thinks he will be back in five or six months, but I don't want him to go."

"He's a good man, Emma, and I want to remind you that getting married is not verboten here. It is just that Father Rapp thought the Society would need much money for our travel to Jerusalem for the Second Coming of our Lord. Women who married might soon have swollen bellies, and then they would not be worth much as workers. If we lost workers, we lost their earnings. It seemed to make sense back then. But never was marrying verboten, just discouraged."

I laid my head against Mama's shoulder. "I've cried so much lately, Mama, that if my tears flow to the river, the river will rise."

"Broken hearts and injured ankles can cause that."

Mama said no more and I found it unnecessary to volunteer anything except, "I love him, Mama. And he loves me. When he returns, we will marry."

"You have my blessing. Let me be the first to tell Yurgen. Later you should talk to him."

As we walked back to the house neither of us spoke. I think Mama was silently preparing for her talk with Papa. I was silently reliving yesterday.

———

Papa was sitting at the table in the common room across from Frederick. They were intently studying the paper on the table. Mama and I started to turn back. "No," Papa said. "Come and see."

There before us, dated May 11, 1824, was the draft of an advertisement offering the entire town of Harmonie for sale. Things could not be much more certain than that. We were leaving Indiana. Papa had several copies of the draft made so he could post them in several places. One of those drafts is included here:

VALUABLE PROPERTY FOR SALE

The following very Valuable property belonging to the Harmonie Society is now by them offered for sale, and is well worthy the attention of Capitalists.

The Town of Harmonie with 20,000 Acres of first rate Land adjoining now offered for sale is situated on the East Bank of the big Wabash, 70 Miles by Water from its Mouth in Posey County State of Indiana and is only 15 Miles by Land from the Ohio River, the Wabash is navigable for many Miles above Harmonie at all seasons for boats of 20 tons burthen, and a great part of the year for Steam boats of the Middle Class.

Amongst the many of improvements on this property may be enumerated the following — There are about 2000 Acres of Land in a high state of Cultivation, 15 of which is in vineyard 35 Acres in Apple Orchard containing about 1500 bearing apple & pear trees all of choice fruit and several considerable peach orchards and gardens of pleasure with a Variety of bearing and ornamental trees in it-one large 3 story Water Merchant Mill with 3 pair of stones, 1 pair of which are French burs, this mill is propelled by a Bayou of the Wabash called the big cutoff. An extensive factory for Cotton & Woolen goods with all the necessary buildings for dying and dressing broad cloths, flannels etc. Two saw Mills, one oil & hemp mill, one large Brick Church 125 by 130 feet, and a frame ditto 55 by 80 feet with Steeples. A 2 story large Brick Store & Stone a warehouse, two large granaries one of which is of Stone, A large tavern house with convenient Kitchen & stabling for the same, — 6 large frame buildings used as mechanics shops, One tanyard of 50 Vates, with barkhouse curriers shop and other necessary buildings attached thereto — three frame Barns of 50 by 100 feet each, with one large & complete threshing machine thereto-3 large sheep stables-6 two story Brick dwelling houses of about 60 feet square each-forty convenient 2 story Brick & frame dwellings of Various sizes, & 86 Log ditto—do-all the dwellings have kitchens with convenient stabling and gardens planted with a variety of choice fruit trees & 2 large distilleries & 1 Brewery with malt kiln &c. The whole of the foregoing property is well supplied with never failing wells & springs of very good water and a number of running streams. The adjoined Country is now thickly Inhabited and there is a great demand for all kinds of Mechanics and for Manufactured Articles generally. -for terms of sale which will be liberal Apply to J .Sons Merchant Philae. Or to A. Way & Co. Merchants Pittsburgh Pa. or to the subscriber living on the premises.

FREDK. RAPP
Agent for George Rapp & Society

Although rumors had been flying like bats around night lights, I was stunned when the events actually happened. There it was, laid out on our table in black and white — Property for Sale.

Harmonie, Indiana, my own little world was for sale.

———•———

I passed Kat's house on the way to find John. She was sitting out in their garden among the flowers doing needle work. "Have you heard the news, Kat?" I asked her.

"What news?"

"That it is true about Harmonie going to be sold. I saw the newspaper draft just a bit ago. I'm not sure that I am making much sense right now. My mind is not doing good thinking for me. There is something else you don't know, Kat. I just couldn't bring myself to tell you. I believe I thought that if I didn't talk about it, I could pretend that it wasn't so. John is leaving. Going back to Italy to take care of some business. He's coming back of course, but he might be gone six months."

"Then by the time he comes back, we may be in Pennsylvania? Is that what you're saying?"

I nodded.

"What are you going to do, Em?"

"I'm going to find a quiet place and think. Right now, I am going to find John and tell him the news. Maybe after I talk to him, the answer will come to me. I'll talk to you again soon, Kat. How are you feeling, you and Thurben and Sophie?"

"We are all surviving, Em. If I did not believe beyond a doubt that I would see my precious Will again in the hereafter, it would be unbearable. You give my greetings to John."

"Yes," I replied and continued on my way.

It did not take long for me to locate John. He was help-ing Solomon clean up some of the construction debris from the house he was building.

"Hello, Emma," Solomon said. "How are your folks?"

"Fine, Solomon. You are going to be finished here be-fore long. It's an especially fine house. Can you spare John for a short time?"

"Of course. Anything for you, Emma. Take all the time you want."

Strange that Solomon would say that. Take all the time you want? If I really took all the time I want, I would have to... Oh, well. As Mama said from time to time when hav-ing one of her spiritual insights, just watch the door. If it remained closed, that was the answer. If it opened, walk through and see what was on the other side.

"I know why you are here and what you want to talk about," John told me when we moved a bit beyond Solomon's house. "The Society is moving back to Pennsyl-vania. Let me give you the answer you are searching for, Cricket. If you want to stay here, do that. Maybe you will like the new people who buy the town. But if you want to leave with your family, then do that. It does not matter at all. Don't you know, my love, that wherever you are, I will find you? I have something that I want to talk about also. I was going to wait until tomorrow, but since we are together, I want to tell you that my boat will be here in two days. I want you to come down to the river to see me off."

John was waiting when I got to the river. "Come here," he said. "You're so lovely that it makes me ache."

My eyes must have glistened because John said, "You know, don't you, that tears will spoil those sparkling blue eyes. Let the last thing I remember be one of your beauti-ful smiles. Think about the wonderful times awaiting us when I get back and smile. There, that's better," he said as

I forced a smile to surface. "Now just let me stand here and look at you for a minute. I want to burn the image of you into my mind. It's already in my heart. I love you so much. You do know that, don't you?"

"I know that, and there are no words in our language to tell you how much I love you."

"You won't forget our love will you, Cricket? Promise me."

"I promise. I won't ever forget. Not ever."

With the tips of his fingers he traced my eyebrows and my lips, gently closed my eyes and kissed one eyelid, then the other. Then he engulfed me in his arms. "I can hardly bear to let you go," he said in a ragged voice. I could feel his heart pounding with mine. Then he kissed me full on the lips, a kiss tender and lingering, a kiss I will feel forever.

Abruptly he turned and, never looking back, hurried to the river and the boat that was waiting to take him away.

———————

The town crier goes through town at nine o'clock, again at midnight, and finally at three o'clock. I heard him as I slid beneath my covers.

Again a day is passed and a step nearer our end. Our time runs out and the joys of Heaven are our reward. Nine strokes and all is well.

Sleep came grudgingly. Mostly I lay awake listening to every sound. A mouse scurried across the floor. Across the hall Papa snored softly. Mama was asleep downstairs. Wolf, the treadmill dog, began to howl. I wanted to howl with him. I wanted to run through the town and through the orchards until I dropped. Why did I feel such foreboding? John would be back in six months or so.

One good thing came from all the thinking, all the tossing and turning, I had definitely decided one thing for sure.

I was not going to Pennsylvania. And the town crier called again.

Harken unto me all ye people, twelve o'clock sounds from the steeple! Twelve gates has the city of God. Blessed is he who enters the fold. Twelve strokes, and all is well.

I pleaded for the sun to come up soon. Surely I would feel better after the sun came up. Things always seemed worse when it was dark. The crier soon told me I had a while to wait.

Again a day has come, our time runs away, and the joys of Heaven are our reward. Three o'clock and all is well.

All is well?
Nothing is well.

PART III

❖ Summer 1824 ❖

Mama, Papa, and Gus were in the first group to leave Indiana. It was May 24, 1824, when they left on the steamboat *Plough Boy*. On the backside of the open stairs in Dormitory Two, someone used chalk to write a parting message in German. In English it said:

In the 24ᵗʰ day of May, 1824, we have departed. Lord, with Thy great help and goodness, in body and soul, protect us.

Papa said they would arrive in Pennsylvania in about two weeks if all went well and that they would post a letter to let us know they had arrived safely. The men who were leaving embraced and kissed those who were staying, first on one cheek and then the other. The women assured each other that they would soon be reunited, some tentatively touching the shoulder or hand of the other. Who dreamed up these customs? Why did the women not hug? Why did they not kiss on the cheeks? When Kat leaves for Pennsylvania, I know I will miss her terribly, so I intend to hug her no matter what anyone says. Maybe no one will say anything. Maybe women have always wanted to say goodbye with an embrace, but didn't want to be the first to break the custom.

My heart ached as I walked beside my family in the procession heading toward the river. It seemed to me that my life had become a string of goodbyes. First there was Will, then John, now my family, and before long, Kat and her family would be leaving. There were about seven hundred people plus freight to be moved, a task that would probably take a year or more. Kat and I would have a little time for ourselves before it was her family's turn to leave.

I knew I would miss Gus. He had somehow become twenty years old, a grown man. He grew up fine. Papa and

Mama were proud of him, I could tell, but, of course, they never told him. I, too, was proud of him and told him so when no one else was around. It embarrassed him but also pleased him. I wondered if he would some day want to get married, maybe even have children. I wondered when I would see him again.

I lagged behind on my return to town. I rather dreaded to go back. Everything had changed. I was so deep in thought that I was startled when I heard my name. I looked up to see Kat coming toward me.

"I came to walk home with you," she said. "I hope you don't mind. Are you all right? I guess you can't be too joyful under the circumstances. Maybe we can sit in the orchard for a spell. We can do whatever you want. Maybe we could..."

"Kat. Shush. It will be alright. One way or another, it will be alright."

"Em, I still don't understand why you didn't go with them. I know John is coming back, but he'll be coming from Italy, and he'll arrive on the East Coast. You would be closer if you were in Pennsylvania."

"Kat, I don't feel like discussing it right now. I want to talk about frivolous things, unimportant things."

She smiled. "That's fine with me. Those are my favorite subjects."

—————

"Are you getting settled in?" Kat asked me when she stopped by a couple of days later.

"I guess you could call it that. What is happening? Our world is spinning out of control, and I'm having trouble hanging on. I'm even queasy in the stomach."

"I've wondered the same thing," Kat answered. "I've stayed awake nights thinking about it. We keep repeating the same thing over and over. First Pennsylvania, then here in Indiana, and now back to Pennsylvania. It isn't often that a group of people build a town, then sell the whole town and build another one far away. That is strange enough but to sell the second town and go back to the original starting place..."

"Well, one thing I have noticed is that things changed after we got the town built," I said. "I think there was more contentment when we were working so hard that we didn't have time to be dissatisfied. We didn't even have time to think about it. We got up, did the work that needed to be done, and went to bed."

"We ate," Kat smiled. "Don't forget that. Remember the brother who left the Society and then wrote to Father Rapp begging to come back? He said they only ate three times a day where he was."

"I remember," I answered, as we both collapsed in laughter. "What a reason to change one's life. To eat more. What do you suppose he said exactly?"

Maybe he just said, "I'm hungry. I want to come back so I can eat." And we burst out laughing again.

The conversation was not particularly humorous, and the stress that produced it could have as easily produced tears. Laughter was better. I wondered if Kat knew yet when she would be leaving, but I could not bear to ask and change the moment.

"Look, Kat," I said. "That lone little flower over there. How do you suppose it got there by itself?"

She took a fleeting glance at the flower and went on with her own conversation. "I think Father Rapp decided that things were not running as smoothly as they once did, mostly because our people had too much time on their hands once the town was completed," she mused. "And you remember all the discussions about the hot, damp weather and the malaria, and the troublesome neighbors."

I didn't answer. I was still looking at the little blue flower. I wondered if the little flower only appeared to be sparkling in the sunshine when actually it was struggling to survive.

"Maybe it's just normal for things to change. Maybe life is like the seasons. Always changing," I said.

"Well, I don't think I like that," Kat answered. "It's unsettling. When things stay the same, you know what to expect. Goodness, we definitely are not talking about frivolous and unimportant things."

"Maybe we are and don't know it," I told her.

"That doesn't sound like you, Em," she said.

"Oh, pay no attention," I replied. "This is not the best day of my life. I really am queasy. I think I need to go back."

I crossed over to Main Street and greeted Christoph at the door of the hospital. Suddenly my legs felt weak. "Christoph, I feel as if..."

I woke to find myself on a hospital bed. "What happened?" I asked.

"Your face suddenly paled," he said. "Then you collapsed and I carried you in here. I think you just have dyspepsia. I'm going to give you a moderate dose of subnitrate of bismuth. You stay here all night, and in the morning I'll see what another sun has brought us. I think you probably have been working too hard. Just rest until tomorrow."

I actually was a bit glad that I was at the hospital where Johanna, Christoph's wife, would be close by so I could call to her if I needed her. When I started to get up, my stomach seemed to turn upside down again. By lunch I felt better.

"Kat came while you were sleeping, and when she comes back later today, she can walk with you to your room," Christoph said. "Don't do much today. Just get caught up on some rest. I'll be close by if you need me."

I was staying in the building behind the hospital. Christoph called it a room, but people live in a house, not a room, so it's a house to me. It once held equipment and supplies for the hospital, but Solomon moved the few things left there into the hospital and in their place installed a stove, and from the community store he also brought a wash stand, a basin, and a bed with covers. He put pegs on the wall for my clothes. One of the community pumps was only a few steps away.

I saw Kat's startled expression at her first visit after I moved in. "It's all right for temporary," I said. Then I remembered hearing those words before. They came from Mama. I was thinking of that first house Mama, Papa, Gus and I had lived in when we first came to Indiana. Now I had to smile when I remembered that four people lived in that one room. I guess for one person this is a spacious living place. And it does not have a dirt floor.

"You should stay with us," Kat said.

It was not long after my collapse that Kat came to tell me the news. "Let's walk down to the orchard," she said. Finally she choked out the words, "A boat, the *Bolivar*, has become available," she said. "We will be sailing much sooner than we thought."

"What does much sooner mean?" I almost shouted. "How much sooner?"

"I don't know exactly, but soon," she said quietly.

We parted company at the big oak, clinging together like little children. I had counted on Kat to be with me. Not since that dreadful time on the *Aurora* had I felt so alone. I was just a few days short of five years old then and completely vulnerable. That's how I felt now.

Although I was extremely tired, I went to the hospital to help Christoph. When I went back home, I left my journal open on the little table on which he used to write out prescriptions that he wanted to remember. He kept meticulous records that noted whether his formulas worked or not and how he might need to adjust the dosage the next time.

Later that evening Christoph tapped softly at my door. He stood silent for a moment then he said, "You forgot your journal, Em."

Words were swimming about in my head, but I couldn't put them together into a comment.

Christoph shuffled from one foot to the other and then finally stammered, "I'm sorry. I couldn't help but read a bit of the page where the book lay open. I still gave no response. "I'm... I'm glad you did the journal," he finally stammered. "Get some rest. Everything's going to be all right." He returned the book to me and left.

Having Christoph by my side would not be the same as having Kat. I knew that he would be there nevertheless, that he would not leave me alone. I put the journal away. I would not be writing in it for a long time.

PART IV

❧ Winter 1824 ❧

Emma was glad to be busy. Some of the Harmonist brothers and sisters would still be there until their time to leave, which depended mostly upon getting an available boat. Until that time life went on as usual, and she helped wherever she was needed. People still came to see Christoph if they had an ailment, and she helped package and dispense herbs, and if someone had a cut that was not too severe, she knew how to cleanse and treat it with ointments that Christoph had developed for such occasions. Since most doctors were educated through the apprenticeship system, it occurred to Emma that if she were a man, the knowledge gained through helping Christoph might have eventually enabled her to be a doctor herself.

Christoph told some entertaining stories as they worked together in the hospital cleaning the rooms, bottles, shelves and tables. One story that she remembered well and still smiled when she thought about it was that some students in Germany sang a song about a doctor Eisenhart, who roamed the countryside practicing medicine according to his own creative methods. Their song said that after he was finished with his treatments, the lame could see and the blind could walk again.

The medical practices of the day usually dictated extreme measures. Emetics were prescribed for anything from a headache to a stomach ailment. However, when compared to other doctors, Christoph was moderate with his prescriptions. For his selection of a cathartic, he used castor oil, which was less harsh than most of the others. He only occasionally used a blistering plaster, a wrap covered with antimony salve and applied to the neck or stomach. They believed the heat would draw the illness out.

Cutting to cause bleeding was intended to let the sickness drain out of the body and was customary with most doctors, but never did Emma see Christoph resort to that method. He commented one day that some doctors' treatments promised that if the person did not die of the disease, he would die of the cure.

Because the Harmonists grew vegetables and fruits and had hogs, cows, sheep, and chickens, they had a varied diet that made them unusually healthy for the time, so Christoph could not make a living by being a doctor exclusively, but since he was an educated man, he could fill in with other avocations. Sometimes he composed and published his own songs and sometimes he directed the band. He also taught school and even served as superintendent for a time. He did research in chemistry and botany and developed methods of food preservation. Emma thought herself lucky to have the tutelage of Yohann Christoph Mueller.

She had walked down to the orchard to have her lunch and was startled to see flowers on the tables because Frederick was in Pennsylvania. It helped her loneliness a bit, no matter who put them there. She could pretend for a moment that things were back as they once were. She caught a glimpse of the large gourds with a hole carved into the side to provide nesting places for the purple martins. The brothers had fastened three wooden cross bars to a tall post and from the end of each of the bars, a gourd swayed gently in the breeze. Encouraging the bird's residency was worth the effort because they kept the mosquitoes and other insects cleared out. Emma loved watching them swoop after the bugs and catch them in flight. After the hatchlings broke free of the eggs, they could have bug meals each day. The birds came every spring but she knew they would soon be gone. She reached into her apron pocket, got her little book, and recorded her thoughts.

Their dawn song filled the air throaty and melodious.

Without looking

I knew the beautiful birds

—with feathers so black they sometimes looked blue—-

had returned.

Without pondering

I knew their stay would be brief and one day

they would leave for their mystery trip far, far away.

They could not stay and I could not go.

She walked back across town to Main Street and was back at work packing boxes of supplies when she heard someone call from outside the door.

"Emma! Another steamboat has arrived. It just came in from Terre Haute. Do you want to go with me to see it?"

Emma stepped from behind the stacked boxes and saw Maria Beisser standing there. "If we hurry, they will let us go aboard and look around. Later we can help with packing and loading," Maria said.

The arrival of a boat was exciting news. If they wanted to travel the river, not only did they have to wait for a boat to be available, but they had to wait for the river to cooperate also. Sometimes it was too high or too low, and sometimes it was frozen.

Emma looked at Christoph and back to Maria. "I don't know if..."

"Yes, Emma, do go. You really need to get away for a spell," Christoph told her.

Emma knew that Maria was out and about much more than she was and would catch her up on all the happenings, and she surprisingly found herself anxious to hear the news. She had been in a self-imposed isolation, living in her tiny little world which had shrunk even more and included mostly the hospital and her living quarters behind it. The only other life she had was the dreams she dreamed at night. She dreamed about the squabbling she and Gus had done, which was the way they had shown their affection for one another. She missed Gus. Sometimes she dreamed about mending days with her mama and their long talks. She dreamt of watching her papa at work and marveling at how kind and thoughtful such a strong man could be. But the last dream she had, she did not want to repeat. She dreamed about John, but she could not remember his face.

Emma and Maria chatted as they walked toward the river. Emma had seen the *Plough Boy* that took her family away but she had seen it only from the river bank. She didn't know what things looked like on board. Because she hadn't yet heard from Gus, she didn't know what the trip had been like. This boat would accommodate twenty people in the cabin and they would have the use of the cabin furniture. They would take their own provisions and do their own cooking on the deck. She supposed the *Plough Boy* had similar rules.

She knew that some of the brothers and sisters had decided to use horses and wagons to go overland to Pennsylvania, perhaps because of the uncertainty of a ship's arrival or maybe just because they preferred horses instead of steam.

"I would be willing to wait quite a while for a boat like that instead of bouncing all the way to Pennsylvania in a wagon, wouldn't you?" Emma asked Maria as they started back to town.

Maria smiled. "I would, but not everyone feels the same way. Mama, for one, is not that fond of the water. In fact she hates it and imagines hundreds of ways that she might meet her demise while on board a steamboat. I have heard her mention that with the roll of the boat she might get dizzy and fall off. I told her that she didn't need to stand on the deck. Later she told my papa that a drooping tree limb might knock her off as the boat passed under it. When he presented logical arguments as to why that would undoubtedly not happen, she decided that a strong wind might rise up unexpectedly and blow her off. I feel quite sure that we will be among those bouncing our way to Pennsylvania."

"I think you are right," Emma laughed. "Anyway, I overheard that they both might travel at about the same speed given all the mishaps that will probably occur both on the river and on land, and that means they might encounter each other along the way. If they do, I would imagine that they will stop and have a celebration meal together."

"That sounds pleasant. And I guess it doesn't matter how we get there, just that we do," Maria replied. "It will be a long time before all of us are settled in. Do you realize that although we, of course, leave all the buildings when we depart, we do take all of the provisions, our tools, and our factory-made things. I guess everything that is loose. That's a lot that has to be packed up and loaded. I don't know about the livestock. Do we take the livestock or did we sell them with the town?"

"I don't know," Emma answered. "I guess I hadn't thought about it. Tomorrow I will start helping Christoph pack some of his books and the supplies he doesn't use often. He will leave in the last boat, but as you already know, no one knows when that will be. This is where I need to leave you. Thanks for stopping by, Maria. I'm sure I will see you again soon. It's been a pleasant afternoon."

And Emma sincerely meant her words. In fact, until now, she had not realized how easy it was to give in to one's feelings and become shut off from the world. She vowed not to let that happen again.

She now thought she knew what Mama meant when she would say something about someone, like, "She's wallowing in her misfortune." She would take her an offering of apple pie or some other treat. Mama never asked any questions as to what brought on the wallowing or that she even noticed it. She just arrived with a smile and a pie.

Emma remembered when they had passed the hog pen one day and a sow, grunting and snorting, had just flopped down in the mud and turned, twisted, rolled and seemed to try to get herself totally covered in the sticky, smelly stuff. "She's wallowing," Mama said as she pointed to the sow. "Wallowing in the filthy mud." But the sow soon stood up, shook herself, and went over to mingle again with the others. Emma decided that maybe there is a time to wallow and then a time to stand up and move back into the world.

She was glad for the boat and for Maria who took her to see it. She spent more time with Maria occasionally and wondered why she had not gotten better acquainted with her sooner because she liked her. But as with everything else, that also ended. She helped Maria and her family pack their things and walked with her to the boat. She watched until it was lost from sight and then walked slowly back to her house.

Christoph met her with good news. He had received a letter from Frederick and as was the custom, other letters had been enclosed, one from Gus, one from Kat and one from Maria. All for Emma. She read the one from Gus first. It was the longest.

Pennsylvania, June 1824

My dear sister,

I know you will want to know about our travel to Pennsylvania. I will tell you about that first.

After leaving you at four o'clock Monday, May 24, we entered the Ohio, forty-eight miles away, at ten o'clock. With

all the hurry we forgot to plan for sleeping that first night and were quite un-
comfortable. First we stood, then we sat,
then we tried to lie down. You can be assured that we were prepared the next
night.

The next day we passed Mt. Vernon and
then Evansville. It must have been about
one o'clock. The day after that everything
went well until at midnight when they
had to take on six cords of wood. Someone said that the Luisiana, a large
steamboat, sped by but I was asleep. Also
during the night, the river fell six feet.
We had to disembark and walk the two
miles to Louisville. The men attached a
rope and pulled the boat along. We were
hoping nothing else bad would happen,
but Friday the pilot ran too close to the
bank, hit a fallen tree, and broke the
shaft and paddles. It was good that we
had such good carpenters along because
we had the boat fixed and on her way
soon. Papa did not feel well, but you
know he would be out there helping get
things fixed anyway. Although rain was
coming down in sheets and continued
to pound us during the night until our
clothes were wet, our beds were wet, and
we were miserable, no one made any
complaints.

Saturday, May 29, we passed Cincin-
nati, Ohio, but the city was up on banks
so high that we could not see it. Sunday
morning the Pennsylvania steamed by.
The next day was uneventful. Father
Rapp said he judged there would be a
total of seven more transports that would

be a repeat of all our adventures or have similar ones.

On Monday, May 31, we passed Gallipolis, Ohio. We were here ten years ago, but I hardly remember it. Tuesday the water was five feet and we scraped the bottom from time to time. It rained some more, and we hoped the water level would rise.

Wednesday was not a good day. For some reason the river, instead of rising, had fallen even more and was now only four and a half feet. We had to fasten a cable to trees and wench the boat along. We ran out of wood and had to gather enough from the forest to last until we reached the next wood yard.

Thursday, the boat was still struggling to move itself along. Almost all of the men were at the front which made the boat go aground, so they quickly ran to the back and that freed it. But even lower waters were ahead, and we went aground again. We were stuck in an industrial town and had to listen to the wild noise and what Father Rapp called debaucheries. He said we were surrounded by untamed people.

On June 4 the river was still low, and we realized we would have to unload to some keel boats. Much of the day was spent unloading Plough Boy and then loading the keel. By evening the keel was on its way with eleven passengers and some of the provisions. With part of the weight gone, our boat could pull the other keel, and we would be on our way.

We had not enjoyed being close to that town.

Saturday, June 5, was uneventful.

June 6, we heard a cannon shot and saw a man waving a white banner. It was Peter Schreibe, the scout, letting us know we were at our final destination and should pull in and unload, which we did. Then the boat headed out for Pittsburgh, which was not too far away, and we headed up the hill to see where our new town was to be.

Papa is still not his usual self but is improving. Mama and I will be glad when Christoph gets here. We hope you also will be on his boat. We all miss you. Kat has enclosed a note, and I know she will tell you about the woman things going on, which I know nothing about.

I send greetings. So do Mama and Papa. We wait anxiously to see you.

Gus

Christoph came into the hospital just as Emma had started her day's work. "Did your letter from Frederick tell about their trip up the river?" Emma asked.

"No," Christoph answered. "My letter was mostly business. Did you get some of the travel news? Did things go well for them?"

"Sometimes," Emma smiled and handed him Gus's letter. "Here, take Gus's letter. It will fill you in on all the happenings. You can give it back to me tomorrow."

"Thanks. How are you feeling?"

"Fine most of the time."

"Emma…"

She waited.

"You're like one of my family, Emma. If you need me, day or night... well, I have this bell. Put it by your bed and if you need me, ring it. If you are in your room and I am in the hospital, I will hear it. I'll have to think of something else if I'm at home."

"Thank you, Christoph. Everything will be all right." Emma smiled as she read the short note from Maria.

Pennsylvania, Winter 1824

Emma,

Mama did not drown. I knew you would be relieved to know that. The Owen group went aground in their keelboat when they got close to our new location and did not know how to dislodge. Our new community was only a few miles away, and when Father Rapp heard about it he sent men to help them. One of the women was crying and could not eat her breakfast because she was so distraught. It must have been dreadful to see the fancy hair in wet straggles and the ruffled dress muddy and torn. These are people from another world. When they started out, most of the women didn't even know how to fix the food or clean the boat, but I am told that some began to look upon the trip as an adventure and learned how to cook simple things and a few even helped row. Maybe they have stronger spirits than I first thought.

Since I am not there to help you pack to come here, I will help you unpack when you arrive. Hurry while I still have the desire.

Maria

Sometimes Maria's comments that she meant as humor sounded a bit sharp. Her mama was always calling her attention to that, but Emma knew that after you really got acquainted you understood that she meant the comment lightly. On the other hand, her mama was right too, but Maria was still quite young and had plenty of time to learn Father Rapp's teachings. Emma liked her and would always remember that she came into her life when she was really needed and she was grateful for that.

Throughout the day Emma felt of the note from Kat tucked safely away in her apron pocket. Reading it was the first thing she did when she got home—in the privacy of her own dwelling.

Emma,

You no doubt wonder what I do every day. Sometimes after the house chores, I help drive the cows to pasture and help bring them back that evening. I don't do that every day, but I take my turn. Some of the time goes to preparing a home for those who are yet to arrive. Our activity is almost a repeat of what we did when we built the town in Indiana. This town has been named Oekonomie or Economy in English. Father Rapp says this new location is the most healthful place he has ever seen, so I guess that means no more malaria.

Two families of free Negroes joined us and are as welcome as they always were in our Society in Indiana. The men in here have again paid their fines for refusing to join the military. As you can see, things are about the same as ever.

You may have been told about the Owen group becoming stuck. The interesting thing was that they were stuck in Safe Harbor Station.

Not really so safe I think. Your new doctor, Dr. Price, fell overboard and crashed into water up to his neck, but he is alright. Robert Dale Owen, Dr. Price, and some others went hunting. There is much game: partridges, pheasants, pigeons, squirrels and deer. The men were such novices that they came back with nothing. One man was seriously injured when he fell over a fence and hit his head on a log. Some of the people left the boat, purchased horses and wagons, and headed out overland. To pass the time, the people on the stranded boat sang and danced on deck, played games of cards, and read. Charles Lesueur spent time sketching. You will probably get to see his work when he gets there. Eventually, the boat was freed and the people were again on their way to Indiana.

My heart is heavy because you are so far away, and I cannot be any help to you. My thoughts are with you each day.

Kat

Emma read the last lines of Kat's letter over and over. She knew Kat would be with her if she could. Gradually she fell back into the habit of not going beyond the hospital and her house. Christoph kept her pretty much informed about the goings and comings of the people: Harmonists going, the Owen's group coming.

One particular morning, Thursday, November 26, Johanna came to the hospital ahead of Christoph. "Emma, Christoph wanted me to talk to you about something," she said solemnly. "He found a newborn baby at the hospital yesterday. I forgot to ask where he found it. Maybe in a box somewhere. Maybe on the steps. Anyway, some poor unfortunate and desperate girl who didn't know what else to do must have left it here and fled. Christoph wanted me to ask you if you would be willing to care for the wee one until we decide what to do."

The baby was a boy, and Emma named him Yohann Gustaf. The first name Yohann was Christoph's name. The middle name Gustaf she borrowed from her brother, Gus. She called the baby Yanni.

Christoph made him a beautiful cradle with Yanni engraved across the top. Johanna embroidered a coverlet and made a pillow of flannel stuffed with cotton. She also brought a stack of crib--sized flannel blankets, towels, and wash-cloths she had made.

Christoph and Johanna were her teachers. They taught her about the baby's feeding, his bathing, and his changing. Johanna even wrote a little book about infant care for Emma to use after they were gone. Their help was tremendously important and useful.

❧ Autumn 1827 ❧

Time rushed by and before she knew it the last boat, the *William Penn*, was loading. Christoph and Johanna were among those boarding. Emma refused to go. "It's too dangerous for Yanni," she said. "I definitely will come later. I have written notes, Christoph. Will you carry them?" He nodded as he reached out and took the notes and after a slight hesitation, he headed toward the river. Emma turned back, passed through the hospital and into her house. How had a year passed so quickly? Actually it had been thirteen months.

The new doctor would arrive soon and she would help him with whatever tasks he thought her capable. If nothing else, she could do the cleaning. If he wanted her for neither, she would think of something else. She had enough provisions to last a long time, but not indefinitely. She could, of course, grow a garden in the spring, but she had no cellar for storage. Christoph had arranged for her to stay in the little building behind the hospital for as long as she needed to, but she thought that probably did not mean forever. Her world was gone, and that included her people. There was a lump in her throat the size of a keelboat.

Yanni looked up from his place on the floor, smiled at her, and continued to try to pick up a piece of sunshine that danced around him. A soft knock sounded at her door. When she opened it, she could tell by the way the woman standing there was dressed that she was one of the Owen's group. "I guess you are Emma," the woman said. "Johanna told us about you and your kindness in taking the orphaned child. I just wanted to introduce myself and tell you that if I can help you, I want you to let me know. Also I will check in from time to time. My name is Frances Wright."

Emma was grateful for the short visit. Such a small gesture, but for some reason, it gave her a sense of belonging. Not that she did belong, but now at least she felt comfortable enough to speak to Frances and even to any of the others that she and Yanni passed on the street. Most would stop to say a few words to Yanni, who turned on his bright smile for everyone. She beamed when compliments came his way. She silently agreed; he was a striking child.

She still hadn't forgotten her first impression of Frances with the soft curls framing her face, her frock revealing her white shoulders a bit, clinched at the middle to emphasize a tiny waist. Emma had looked down at her own loosely fit garment that masked any kind of a woman's figure that might have been present. She envisioned herself with the soft curls and the stylish garment,but to dwell on that was such a frivolous thing. The important thing was that she liked Frances.

The more that Emma was among the Owenites, the more she began to learn their ways. They were very different from her people. One strange thing she noticed was that Robert Dale Owen and Frances Wright were not married but they traveled together. She was sure that it was because Robert Dale needed to take care of Frances during her sick spells, but still that would have been frowned upon with her people. Another thing was that Owenites opposed any use of alcohol to drink, even drinking beer and wine in moderation with meals. They could hardly believe the drunkenness that went on among the villagers.

The Owenites had renamed her town and now called it New Harmony. That was an appropriate name because the town certainly was new to her. She was fascinated, especially by the new ideas in education. They called it the Pestalozzian method. It promoted learning by doing as opposed to learning by memorization.

Because Dr. Price was a bit crotchety and hardly ever needed her, she readily accepted a job assisting some of the teachers. She taught embroidery, Harmonist cooking, baking, and growing herb gardens. The Owenite women were fascinated by the fact that planting tansy by the doors would help keep the flies away.

The main thing different in this New Harmony place was all of the quarreling between William Maclure and Robert Owen. They both had invested heavily in time and money to get this community organized, but they agreed about almost nothing. Maclure's School of Industry started the trade school idea, but after that he asked that his investment money be returned and he left. Not long afterward Robert Owen went back to Scotland. Emma wondered how he thought a community could run itself. He must have, however, because he spent most of his time away promoting his new ideas of education and how he wanted to equalize power and property for the new communities that he wanted to develop. He hoped his philosophy would spread all over the world. Another problem in management was that anyone could move into New Harmony without being screened as they had been when Father Rapp was there. The new community collected people of various philosophical, religious, and political beliefs and that caused even more conflict. Robert Dale helped start free public schools for both males and females, a good thing, and Frances was an avid disciple of antislavery. Although good things were happening, the community was rapidly falling apart.

Frances still had frequent bouts of sickness, and when she had one episode that was worse than others, Robert Dale decided to take her back to Europe. Because they would be going to the East Coast to connect with a ship bound for Europe, Emma and Yanni would go with them as far as Economy.

She sent a letter to her family announcing her plan and closed by saying, "I have a three year old child I am bringing with me. His name is Yanni."

PART V

✦ Economy, Pennsylvania ✦

In the distance Emma thought she saw some movement on the hill. As they got closer she could see the white flag and knew it was Peter Schreibe signaling to let them know this was the place to stop. He ran down the hill, grabbed the rope that was thrown to him, and tied up. He assisted Emma and Yanni off the keelboat after they had said their goodbyes to the people onboard, especially Frances and Robert Dale. They watched the boat disappear into the distance and accepted Peter's help up the hill. Although Emma had been told that there was almost a complete town there already, she was still amazed at what she saw. It was as if she had never left Pennsylvania thirteen years ago. The town looked almost the same except for the dwellings. She saw only the six room houses, no dormitories.

A group of people were coming down the street. The three in front were Gerta, Yurgen, and Gus, who was holding onto Yurgen's arm to steady his walk. It is said that the Germans do not show much emotion, but there was plenty of that right there on the street. Gerta didn't appear to be crying, but tears flowed down her face and dripped off her chin. Yurgen could say nothing but, "Emma, Emma." And then he hugged her and held her head against his chest cradled in both of his big, rough hands. Gus grabbed her and swung her around until she was dizzy. And then they all laughed and laughed.

Then she saw Kat patiently waiting her turn. She went over and took both Kat's hands in hers, hesitated only a moment, hugged her, and kissed her on both cheeks. Yanni was pulling on her skirt. "Em," he said. That was all, but his eyes revealed a look of uncertainty akin to fear.

"Oh, Yanni, it's alright. Everything's alright. This is my Mama and Papa and Gus. Gus is my brother. We are not sad, sweet boy. I think we are happier than we have been in years. Everybody, this is Yanni, the love of my life."

It seemed that the whole town gathered that evening out under the stars for singing, Father Rapp's preaching, and, of course, food.

"Isn't it time to start home?" Yurgen asked, and even though it was a bit early, Emma and her family were ready to be by themselves for a while. And Yurgen was visibly tiring.

"Thank you, Emma, for coming back into our lives and for bringing the boy with you," Yurgen said, then added, "I think I'll go upstairs." As he passed Emma he patted her shoulder again and again.

"I'm going, too, Papa," Gus said.

Gerta said Gus did that every night so that Yurgen wouldn't have to ask for help going up the stairs. "Soon Yurgen will have to sleep down here in the common room," she said.

"I wasn't prepared to see Papa like this," Emma told her.

"Your Papa is happier now than I have seen him in years, Emma. He has missed you so much."

"I feel guilty, Mama."

"No, Emma, you mustn't. You did the best you could. We knew that. It's just that we missed you."

Emma nodded. "Alright, Yanni, let's go. Good night, Mama. It's good to be home."

After the long trip and all the excitement, Emma and Yanni almost went to sleep on the way up the stairs.

The next morning Emma looked up as Gus came from upstairs. She could tell something was amiss from his expression. "Gus, what's wrong?" she asked.

Gerta turned around. "Yurgen went on without me, didn't he?? It was more a statement than a question. "Get Father Rapp, Gus," she said.

"Oh, Mama, I'm the one..."

"Don't do that, Emma. He stayed several days longer than he wanted to waiting for you. I will be forever grateful for you getting here on time. It made him so happy."

And in less than a year Gerta went to join her beloved Yurgen.

———•———

Emma stood by herself and watched the river roll by. Gus walked up beside her. "I was wrong, Gus. Things do change. Moment by moment it seems. Like this river."

"You're too philosophical for me, Emma." Emma smiled slightly and took Gus's arm as they walked back up the hill.

"I'm getting married, Em."

"I thought you might be. I'm glad. Make sure you have chosen carefully. Remember Mama and Papa."

"I know, and I think I have chosen well. She reminds me of you, Em."

She looked at him and thought of something teasing to say. Instead she said, "Gus, if I should be taken from this earth on the way home, will you always look after Yanni?"

Gus began to laugh. "Here, let me get a tighter grip on your arm in case you start to float away. "

"If we were children again, a basin of water would be headed your way, young man."

"I will always watch over Yanni, no matter how old he is, and you didn't have to ask. He has had a good upbringing. I don't imagine he will need any help, but if he does..."

"Do you mind, Gus, if I sit here on this bench for a bit? I want to watch the martins. They look so free. Do you wonder what it would be like to fly through the air like that?"

"Actually, Em, I never do."

She poked him with her elbow. "They are getting ready to make their long trip. Where do you think they go?"

"Somewhere nice, I'm sure," Gus said.

———·——

Many years passed. Anymore it seemed that Kat and Emma talked mostly about the past. Most of their conversations began with "Remember when..."

Today it was "Remember when I got lost in the Labyrinth?"

"No. When was that?" Kat asked.

"I guess you don't remember because you were so young."

"We're both the same age!"

"Oh, Yes. That's true. I guess I remember it because it happened to me. I was so afraid."

There was a long silence.

"Are you going to tell me about it?" Kat asked.

"I was trying to remember exactly when it happened. The hedges had grown taller than I was. I had been told not to go in there alone, but I went in there to hide and got my frock caught on a thorn bush. I could not reach around to the back to free myself, and I could not pull loose. It got dark and I could hear people calling for me, but they were too far away to hear me answer. It seemed forever before they found me. I had been sobbing so long that I had lost my voice. Papa carried me home. He kept saying, "It's alright, little one." Mama's eyes were red and swollen."

"What happened the next day?" Kat wanted to know.

"Punishment, you mean? None. Both Mama and Papa believed that when I put myself into situations that became hurtful, that was punishment enough. Because of my experience when I was little, I always thought of my escapade when Father Rapp gave his sermons from the labyrinth. I think I actually thought of that more than the sermon. You won't tell will you?"

"Em, I have so many things I am not supposed to tell, I am going to have to quit talking entirely."

Emma smiled and decided not to reply. Instead she said, "Remember when Yanni first came to Economy? He was almost four and that was how old we were when we arrived at Baltimore," Emma said.

"No. We were almost five. I was anyway," Kat replied.

"Then I guess I was too. I felt so lost. But I had such a wonderful life with Mama, Papa and Gus, and then Yanni."

PART VI

❧ Journey Through a Labyrinth ❧

Emma had been back in Pennsylvania for many years when she noticed that the towns seemed to run together. She gazed at the town pumps for example, and tried to remember if they were in the same location in the Indiana community. And where were the community ovens in Harmonie, Pennsylvania? Wasn't there one on every street? They grew hemp, cut it, and strung the tall herb along the outside edge of the city where they separated the rough fibers. Men walked backward as they twisted it into rope. What side of town was that rope walk on? Emma didn't remember, but the answers really didn't make difference anyway.

Because Emma had helped Christoph so much in Indiana, she went over to the hospital to see if she could help Dr. Herrman with the people here who were sick with consumption. By the time two weeks had gone by, Emma herself was in bed with the illness. When the sun came up the second time, she did not mention going back to work. Dr. Herrman came to the house every day to see her and give her some medicine, but she did not improve.

Kat was sitting quietly by the bed holding Emma's hand when Yanni came. He looked tired and worn. "How is she?" he asked.

"About the same," Kat replied. "She roused enough to take a wee bit of broth and a sip of water, but that was all. I thought she might have tried to smile, but probably not. Probably, I was just hoping."

Kat moved away so that Yanni could take her place. "Em," he said softly as he pushed a wisp of hair back from her face. She stirred then and opened her eyes. This time it was not questionable. She smiled. Certainly not a big smile, but definitely a smile.

"I was happy to hear that you ate some broth, Em. You need to eat. Could you eat some more if I feed it to you?"

But she was again asleep, the image of the smile bathing her face.

Yanni sat down with his elbows propped up on the bed, his face buried in his hands. From a distance he heard Kat's voice. She was talking to someone, but whoever it was did not participate in the conversation. The footsteps became louder and Kat came into the room closely followed by Aldo Bonn. Aldo walked slowly to the bedside and stood as if turned into stone, as if he didn't know what to do now that he was there. Finally, he tentatively reached out and touched the tips of his fingers to the coverlet that covered Emma's frail body. Kat thought she saw his body shudder as he placed an envelope on the bed and still, without a word, he left.

Both Yanni and Kat were silent. "You take it, Kat," Yanni finally said.

There seemed to be two notes. One was from Aldo. It said:

When John's letter came, I volunteered to deliver it. Instead I hid it away. I have brought it now in hopes that it will give her comfort and bring me forgiveness from the Almighty.

The second note, the one that Aldo had hidden away for years said:

Cricket,
Could not board ship. Very sick. Will return when strong enough. Miss you. Will love you throughout all eternity.

John

Kat leaned over close to Emma's ear and excitedly read the words from John's letter. "You see, Em. He didn't marry the Madda person. He was coming back to you, but he got sick."

Emma opened her eyes. "Braid my hair, Kat. I don't want John to see me like this," she said in a raspy whisper. And this time there was no mistake. She smiled one of the wonderful smiles they were used to seeing, then closed her eyes and drifted peacefully into her eternal rest.

Emma was laid to rest next to her Mama and Papa. Gus and Yanni led the procession. Yanni remembered when Gerta died. As he had walked beside Em in that procession, Em had said softly, "Yanni, from the top of my head to the tips of my toes, I completely loved her." At this moment he really understood what she felt.

————+·——

Kat took Yanni back home with her. "I have some things to show you," she told him.

"I saw another paper, Kat. What was it?"

"From the hospital in Italy," she said. "It documents John's serious illness, an illness that led to his death. They had no one else to contact but Emma."

"Kat! She thought he was still alive."

"Yes, she did. And she thought that she was still twenty-four years old."

"Why did you do that? Why did you let her believe that?"

"Did you see her face, Yanni? Did you see the light that came back into her eyes? I knew she had only a brief time to remain with us. I wanted her to be happy when she left. I think she was. Don't you?"

After a brief hesitation, Yanni said, "Yes, I'm sure she was."

We sat in silence. Then Yanni asked, "What was Em like, Kat, before I knew her?"

"She loved to write, and after you came into her life, she wanted her journal to be for you. When she got sick, she told me where to find a special box she had kept. I think she sensed that the outcome of her illness was not going to be good."

Kat opened a drawer and removed the journal that Emma had secured in a beautiful hand-painted box that she herself had painted. On the top, a stallion with a beautiful flowing mane lifted his feet high as he pulled a carriage through the snow. Around the sides the sun shone down on a meadow where dozens of violets sparkled with dew. Kat carefully lifted the lid and removed two yellowed pieces of paper that had been unfolded and folded again many times over. These she handed to Yanni.

On one paper were the words:

Emma, from this day on, you shall not walk alone. I will be with you whether near or far. I will love you with my every breath for all my life and beyond.

And on the other:

John, from this day on, I give you my loyalty and my heart. You are a part of my hopes and dreams. You are my friend and my love completely and forever.

"These sound like marriage vows, Kat."

"That's what they are. Emma and John wrote their own vows and said them to each other before he left. They planned to have Father Rapp perform another more formal ceremony when John returned.

"But he didn't come back."

"No, he didn't," Kat said.

———·——

Yanni took the journal with him and with the aid of a Betty lamp, read far into the night.

He read about Emma's journey across the Atlantic. Such a tiny little girl, he thought, and marveled at her bravery. He smiled at her account of cutting off her braids and laughed out loud at her story about the dueling brooms. He sensed her fear when she thought the dog, Wolf, was one of the invaders who had come back to harm her. In a way he felt surprise that Emma was once young and that she had fallen deeply in love with anyone, let alone someone other than a Harmonist. He found it hard to believe she had exchanged vows with this man, John, in a private ceremony without the knowledge of her parents or anyone else. That in itself revealed her deep feelings for the man and her independent nature.

When he met with Kat the next morning, Yanni carefully placed the box on the table. "Thank you," he said softly. "Was John a good person?"

"Emma loved him," Kat said. "That is the answer."

"Yes, of course," Yanni replied. "What did he look like?"

"Like you," Kat said. "Your hair is light brown and his was dark. Other than that, you look a lot like him." With those words she handed him the hand-painted box. "This is yours. Emma made it for you. I was only entrusted to keep it safe." Then she turned and left the room. Obviously she had talked all she wanted to.

———·——

When he got home, Yanni took Emma's journal out and held it on his lap. He studied the picture of the labyrinth she had drawn on the cover, the confusing paths outlined by bushes and circling the temple of peace in the center.

When dark closed in, he still sat alone, his mind working furiously, trying to put all the pieces together. Trying to make the picture whole. Without getting up he reached over to put the box onto the table across from his chair and lost his grip. Amidst all the jostling, a paper became dislodged from the bottom of the box, flew up into the air, then fell to the floor. He lit a lamp and read from the paper. It was information about his birth. His name was recorded as Yohann Gustaf Donato. Stunned, he leafed through the journal until he again found John's real name. Donato. Now everything came together. Emma and John's private wedding, March 3. A baby boy found at the hospital, Nov. 26, nine months later. He eased himself into a chair. "I was not left at the church in a box. I am Emma and John's son," he said softly.

Yanni thought about Emma and the years it took to create the journal, the years she had kept her secret. Although he had seen her painting the box and had admired it, he had known nothing about its real purpose. He always knew that she loved him, but only now did he know how much. As a parting gift, his beloved Em had removed all his uncertainties and in their place had given him peace.

Exhausted, he slipped into bed and quickly drifted into a deep slumber. Much later, half awake and half asleep, he heard the town crier's call:

Harken unto me all ye people. Three o'clock sounds from the steeple. Time slipped by. Another day is nigh. Three strokes and all is well.

www.ingramcontent.com/pod-product-compliance
Lightning Source LLC
Chambersburg PA
CBHW031836170626
46807CB00004B/1488